# THE ITALIAN'S PREGNANT VIRGIN

BY
MAISEY YATES

MILLS & BOON

First Published in Great Britain 2016
By Mills & Boon, an imprint of HarperCollins*Publishers*
1 London Bridge Street, London, SE1 9GF

© 2016 Maisey Yates

ISBN: 978-0-263-92384-1

Our policy is to use papers that are natural, renewable and recyclable
products and made from wood grown in sustainable forests. The logging
and manufacturing processes conform to the legal environmental
regulations of the country of origin.

Printed and bound in Spain
by CPI, Barcelona

# "The thing is, Mr. Valenti, I'm pregnant."

Renzo Valenti, heir to the Valenti family real estate fortune, known womanizer and chronic over-indulger, stared down at the stranger standing in his entryway.

He had never seen the woman before in his life. Of that he was one hundred percent certain.

He did not associate with women like this. Women who looked like they had spent an afternoon traipsing through the streets of Rome, rather than an afternoon tangled in silk sheets.

Esther was red-cheeked and disheveled, her face void of make-up, long dark hair half falling out of a bun that looked like an afterthought.

Had she been walking by him outside he would never have paid her any notice. Except she was in his home. And she had just said words to him no woman had spoken to him since he was sixteen years old.

But they meant nothing. As she meant nothing.

"Congratulations. Or condolences," he said. "Depending."

"You don't understand—"

"No," he said, his voice cutting through the relative silence of the grand antechamber. "I don't. You practically burst into my home, telling my housekeeper you had to see me, and now here you are, having pushed your way in. Regardless, you're not drawing this out and making a show, and I have no p

"It's

3011780263114 9

**Maisey Yates** is a *New York Times* bestselling author of more than thirty romance novels. She has a coffee habit she has no interest in kicking, and a slight Pinterest addiction. She lives with her husband and children in the Pacific Northwest. When Maisey isn't writing she can be found singing in the grocery store, shopping for shoes online and probably not doing dishes. Check out her website: maiseyyates.com.

### Books by Maisey Yates

### Mills & Boon Modern Romance

*Carides's Forgotten Wife*
*Bound to the Warrior King*
*Married for Amari's Heir*
*His Diamond of Convenience*
*To Defy a Sheikh*
*One Night to Risk it All*

#### Heirs Before Vows

The Prince's Pregnant Mistress
The Spaniard's Pregnant Bride

#### The Chatsfield

Sheikh's Desert Duty

#### One Night With Consequences

The Greek's Nine-Month Redemption
Married for Amari's Heir

#### Princes of Petras

A Christmas Vow of Seduction
The Queen's New Year Secret

#### Secret Heirs of Powerful Men

Heir to a Desert Legacy
Heir to a Dark Inheritance

Visit the Author Profile page at millsandboon.co.uk for more titles.

To my parents, who actually are great
and have always supported me. In spite of
what 90% of my characters' parents might suggest.

# CHAPTER ONE

"THE THING IS, Mr. Valenti, I'm pregnant."

Renzo Valenti, heir to the Valenti family real estate fortune, known womanizer and chronic overindulger, stared down at the stranger standing in his entryway.

He had never seen the woman before in his life. Of that he was nearly one hundred percent certain.

He did not associate with women like this. Women who looked like they had spent a hot, sweaty afternoon traipsing through the streets of Rome, rather than a hot, sweaty afternoon tangled in silk sheets.

She was red-cheeked and disheveled, her face void of makeup, long dark hair half falling out of a bun that looked like an afterthought.

She was dressed the same as many American college students who flooded the city in the summer. She was wearing a form-fitting black tank top and a long, ankle-length skirt that nearly covered her dusty feet and flat, unremarkable sandals that appeared to be falling apart.

Had she been walking by him outside, he would never have paid her any notice. Except she was in his home. And she had just said words to him no woman had said to him since he was sixteen years old.

But they meant nothing, as she meant nothing.

"Congratulations. Or condolences," he said. "Depending."

"You don't understand."

"No," he said, his voice cutting through the relative silence of the grand antechamber. "I don't. You practically burst into my home telling my housekeeper you had to see me, and now here you are, having pushed your way in."

"I didn't push my way in. Luciana was more than happy to *let* me in."

He would never fire his housekeeper. And the unfortunate thing was, the older woman knew it. So when she had let a hysterical girl into his home, he had a feeling she considered it punishment for his notorious behavior with the opposite sex.

Which was not fair. This little *creature*—who looked as though she would be most at home sitting on a sidewalk in the vicinity of Haight-Ashbury, playing an acoustic guitar for coins—might well be some man's unholy punishment. But she wasn't his.

"Regardless, you're not drawing this out and making a show, and I have no patience for either."

"It's *your* baby."

He laughed. There was absolutely no other response for such an outrageous statement. And there was no other way to remove the strange weight, the strange tension that gripped him when she spoke the words.

He knew why it affected him. But it should not.

He could imagine no circumstance under which he would touch such a ridiculous little hippie. And even so, he had just spent the past six months devoted to the world's most obscene farce of a marriage.

And though Ashley had been devoted to the pleasure of both herself—and other men—during their union, he had been faithful.

A woman with a small baby bump, barely showing

beneath that skin-tight top, claiming to be carrying his child could be absolutely nothing but ridiculous to him.

He'd had nothing at all but six months of fights, dodging vases flung in a rage by his crazy wife—who seemed to do her best to demolish the stereotype that Canadians were a nice and polite people—and then days on end of ridiculous cooing like he was some kind of pet she was trying to tame again after a sound beating.

Little realizing that he was not a man to be tamed, and never had been. He had married Ashley to make a point to his parents, and for no other reason. As of yesterday, he was divorced and free again.

Free to take this little backpacker in any way he wanted to, if he so chose.

Though, she would find the only place he wanted to take her was out the front door, and back onto the streets she had come from.

"That, you will find, is impossible, *cara mia*." Her eyes went round, liquid, shock and pain visible. What had she imagined would happen? That he would fall for this ruse? That she would find her salvation in him? "I can see how you would build some strange fantasy around the idea I might be your best bet for help," he said, attempting to keep his tone calm. "I have a reputation with women. But I have also been married for the past six months. So whatever man is responsible for knocking you up in a bar crawling with tourists and never calling again? He is not me, nor will you ever con me into believing it is. I am divorced now, but in the time I was married I was faithful to my wife."

"Ashley," she said, blinking rapidly. "Ashley Bettencourt."

He was stunned, but only momentarily, by her usage of his wife's name. It was common knowledge, so of course if she knew about him, she would know about Ashley. But if she knew he was married, why not choose an easier target?

"Yes. Very good," he said. "You're up on your tabloid reading, I see."

"No, I *know* Ashley. She's actually the person I met in a bar crawling with tourists. *She's* the one who knocked me up."

Renzo felt like he'd been punched in the chest. "Excuse me? None of what you're saying makes sense."

The little woman growled, lifting her hands and gripping her head for a moment before throwing them back down at her sides, curling her fingers into fists. "I am… I am trying. But I thought you would know who I was!"

"Why would I know who you are?" he asked, feeling at a loss.

"I just… Oh, I should never have listened to her. But I was… I am just as stupid as my dad thinks I am!" She was practically wailing now, and he had to admit, this farce was inventive even if it was damned disruptive to his day.

"Right at this moment I'm on your father's side, *cara*, and I will remain so until you have offered me an explanation that falls somewhere short of being as stupid as my *ex-wife* getting you pregnant."

"Ashley hired me. I was working at a bar down by the Colosseum, and she and I started talking. She was telling me about the issues in your marriage and the trouble you were having conceiving…"

The words made his gut twist. He and Ashley had never attempted to conceive. By the time they'd gotten to a place where they might discuss giving him an heir to his empire, he'd already decided that no amount of shock value made her worth it as a wife.

"I thought it was weird, her talking to me like that. But she came back the next night, and the next. We talked

about how I ended up in Italy and how I had no money…"
She blinked. "And then she asked me if I would consider
being her surrogate."

Pressure built in Renzo's chest until it exploded. English deserted him entirely, a string of vulgar Italian flowing from his lips like a foul river. "I don't believe it. This
is some trick that bitch has put you up to."

"It's not. I promise you it isn't. I had no idea that you
didn't know. No idea at all. It was all very… What she
said… It made sense. And…and she said it would be easy.
Just a quick trip to Santa Firenze, where the procedure is
legal, and then I just have to…be the oven. I was supposed
to get paid to make the bread, so to speak, and then…
well, give it to the person I…baked it for. Someone who
wanted the baby desperately enough to ask for help from
a stranger."

Panic tore through Renzo like a wild beast, savaging his
chest, his throat. Making it impossible to breathe. What
she was saying was impossible. It had to be. Mostly.

Ashley was…unpredictable. And God knew how that
might manifest. Especially since she'd been enraged by
the divorce—made simple because of their marriage in
Canada, which she had felt was calculated on his part. It
was, of course.

But she wouldn't have done this. She couldn't have.
Still, he pressed.

"It made sense to you that a woman pursued surrogacy,
and claimed to have a husband whom you never saw?"

"She said that it would be impossible for you to come
to the clinic. She could only do it because she wore large
sunglasses and a hat. She said that you were far too recognizable. She said you were very tall." She swept her hand
up and down. "You are. Obviously. You don't blend. Not
even sunglasses would disguise… You know what I mean."

"I know nothing. It has become apparent to me over the past few minutes that I know less than I thought. That snake talked you into this. How much did she pay you?"

"Well, she hasn't given me everything yet."

He laughed, the sound bitter. "Is that so? I hope that final price is a high one."

"Well, the problem is that Ashley said she doesn't want the baby anymore. Because of the problems that you're having."

"Problems?" The question was incredulous. "Does she mean our divorce?"

"I...I guess."

"So, you did some cursory research on us, and then no more?"

"I don't have internet at the hostel," she said flatly.

"You live in a hostel?"

"Yes," she said, her cheeks turning a darker shade of pink. "I was just passing through. And I ran out of money. Took a job at a bar, and I've been here longer than I anticipated. Then I met Ashley about three months ago."

"How far along are you?"

"Only about eight weeks. I just... Ashley decided she didn't want the baby anymore. And I don't want to...I don't want to end the pregnancy. And I thought that even though she said you didn't want to handle any of this, because it damaged your view of the whole thing...I wanted to come to you. I needed to make sure."

"Why is that? Because you fancy that you will raise the baby if I don't want it?"

It was her turn to laugh. There was no humor in it, only hysteria. "No! I'm not going to raise a baby. Not now. Not *ever*. I don't want children. I don't want a husband. But I was involved in this. I agreed to it. And I feel like...I don't know. How can I not feel responsible? She became a friend to me almost. I mean, she was one of the first people in forever who talked to me, told me about her life. She made sure I knew how much she wanted this baby and…now she doesn't. She might have changed her mind, but I can't change my feelings about it."

"What will you do?" he asked. "What will you do if I tell you I don't want the baby?"

"I'll give it up for adoption," she said, as though it were the most obvious thing. "I was going to give birth anyway. That was part of the agreement."

"I see." His thoughts were racing, trying to catch up with everything that the woman in front of him—the woman whose name he still didn't know—was saying to him. "And was Ashley planning on paying you the rest of the fee if you continued with the pregnancy?"

The woman looked down. "No."

"So, you had to make sure that you could still collect your fee? Is that why you came to speak to me?"

"No. I came to speak to you because it seemed like the right thing to do. Because I was becoming concerned about your lack of involvement in the whole thing."

Anger built inside him, reaching its boiling point and bubbling over. "Allow me to paint a clear picture for you of what exactly happened. My ex-wife went behind my back to hire you. I still don't understand how this happened. I don't understand how she was able to manipulate both you and the doctor. I don't understand how she was able to accomplish this without my knowing. I don't understand what her endgame was, as she is now clearly backing out. Perhaps now that she has seen she will get no money from me, and I'm not worth the effort anyway, she does not wish to be saddled with my child for the rest of her shallow existence. Or, perhaps it is simply Ashley. Who decided to do something on a whim, thinking that something of this magnitude would be a delightful surprise she would drop in my lap like the purchase of a new handbag. And much like my ex feels about handbags, she has decided she is bored of this one and moved on to the next shiny thing. Regardless of her motivation, the end result is the same. I didn't know. I did not want this baby."

At that, she seemed to deflate. Her shoulders shrunk inward, some of her defiant posture diminishing. "Okay." She blinked rapidly, lifting her chin and staring him down. "If you change your mind, I'm at the hostel Americana. You can find me there. Unless I'm working at the bar across the street." She turned on her heel and began to walk away from him, toward the front door. Then she paused. "You claim you've been in the dark this whole time. I just didn't want you to have that excuse anymore."

Then she walked out of his house. And just like his ex-wife, he determined that he would think about her no more.

It nagged at him. There was no escaping it. For three days he'd attempted to ignore and dismiss the events that had occurred earlier. He did not know the woman's name. He didn't even really know if she was telling the truth. Or if she was another of his ex-wife's games.

Knowing Ashley, that was it. Just a game. A weird attempt to try to draw him back into her web. She had been far too content with the dissolution of their union. Particularly after she had been so bitter about it in the first place. She had claimed he had always known it would end this way. Which was why they had sought marriage outside the country. Divorce in Italy was far too complicated. And, he supposed, the fact that he had covered his bases in such a manner was in some ways indicative of his commitment. Or at least, his faith in the mercurial Ashley.

But then, he imagined Ashley had gotten her revenge. Surrogacy was not legal in Italy. Undoubtedly why she had sought to have the procedure done in neighboring Santa Firenze.

More the pity that his sister, Allegra, had dissolved her agreement with the prince of that country and married Renzo's friend—Spanish duke Cristian Acosta, who would be no help to him in this situation—instead.

He should let it go. Likely the woman was lying. Even if she weren't…what should it matter to him?

A sharp pang in the vicinity of his heart told him he clearly hadn't had enough to drink. So, he set out to remedy that. But for some reason, grabbing a hold of the bottle of Scotch reminded him of what the stranger had said before she'd left.

She worked at a bar. She worked at a bar near the Colosseum, and if he wanted to find her he could look there.

He took the stopper out of the Scotch bottle. That would all be very well and good if he in fact wanted to find her. He did not. There was no point in searching for a woman who was—in point of fact—probably only attempting to scam money out of him.

But the possibility lingered. It lingered inside him like an acrid smell that he couldn't shake. One that remained long after the source of the odor was removed. He couldn't let it go because of Jillian. Because of everything that had happened with her.

He gritted his teeth, setting the bottle back down. Then, he strode toward his closet, grabbing a pair of shoes and putting them on quickly. He would get his car, he would go down to the bar, and he would confront this woman. Then, he would be able to come back home and go to bed, sleeping well, knowing with full confidence that she was a liar and that there was no baby.

He paused for a moment, taking a deep breath. Perhaps he was being overly cautious. But given his history, he felt he had to be. He had lost one child, and he would not lose another one.

# CHAPTER TWO

ESTHER ABBOTT TOOK a deep breath as she cleared off the last table of her shift. Hopefully, she would have a decent amount of money in tips when she counted everything up, then, she would finally be able to rest easy. Her feet hurt. And she imagined that as early on as she was in the pregnancy, she couldn't exactly blame it on that.

It was just the fact that she had been working for ten hours. But what other choice did she have? Renzo Valenti had sent her away. Ashley Bettencourt wanted nothing to do with her or the baby. And if Esther had any sense in her head she would probably have complied with the other woman's wishes and pursued a termination. But she just couldn't do it.

Apparently, she had no sense in her head. She had a lot of feelings inside her chest, though. Feelings that made all of this seem impossible, and painful, and just a bit too much.

She had come to Europe to pursue independence. To see something of the world. To try to gain perspective on life away from the iron fist of her father. That brick wall that she could no more reason with than she could break apart.

In her father's world, a woman didn't need an education that extended beyond homemaking. In her father's world, a woman didn't need to drive, not when her husband should accompany her everywhere at all times. In her father's world a woman could have no free thought or independence. Esther had always longed for both.

And it was that longing that had gotten her into trouble. That had caused her father to kick her out of the commune. Oh, she'd had options, she supposed. To give up the "sinful" items she'd been collecting. Books, music. But she'd refused.

It had been so hard. To make that choice to leave. In many ways it had been her choice, even if it was an ultimatum. But the commune had been home, even if it had been oppressive.

A place filled with like-minded people who clung to their version of old ways and traditions they had twisted to suit them. If she had stayed any longer, her family would have married her off. Actually, they would have done it a long time ago if she hadn't been such a problem. The kind of daughter nobody wanted their son to marry.

The kind of daughter her father eventually had to excommunicate to set an example to the others. His version of love. Which was really just control.

She huffed out a laugh. If they could see her now. Pregnant, alone, working in a den of sin and wearing a tank top that exposed a slim stretch of midriff whenever she bent over. All of those things would be deeply frowned upon.

She wasn't sure if she approved of her situation either. But it was what it was.

Why had she ever listened to Ashley? Well, she *knew* why. Because she had been tempted by the money. Because she wanted to go to college. Because she wanted to extend her time in Europe, and because she found that waiting tables really was kind of awful.

There was nothing all that romantic about backpacking. About staying in grimy hostels.

It was more than that, though. Ashley had seemed so vulnerable when they'd met. And she had painted a picture of a desperate couple in a rocky place in their marriage, who needed a child to ease the pain that was slowly breaking them apart.

The child would be so loved. Ashley had been adamant about that. She had told Esther about all her plans for the baby. Esther hadn't been loved like that. Not a day in her life.

She had wanted to be part of that. Even in just a small way.

Finding out that was a lie—the happy-family picture Ashley had painted—was the most wrenching part of it all.

She laughed and shook her head. Her father would say this was her punishment for being greedy. For being disobedient and headstrong.

Of course, he would probably also expect this would send her running back home. She wouldn't do that. Not ever.

She looked up, looked at the view in front of her. Looked around her at the incredible clash of chaos that was Rome. How could she be regretful? It might be difficult to carry the baby to term with no help. But she would. And then after that she would make sure that the child found a suitable home.

Not one with her. But then, it wasn't her baby, after all. It was Renzo's. Renzo and Ashley's. Her responsibilities did not extend beyond gestation. She felt pretty strongly about that.

The hair on the back of her neck seemed to stand on end, a rush of prickles moving down her spine. She straightened, then slowly turned. And through the crowd, across the bar that was teeming with people, tables crammed together, the dark lighting providing a sense of anonymity, he seemed to stand out like a beacon.

Tall, his dark hair combed back off his forehead, custom suit tailored perfectly to his physique. His hands were shoved in his pockets, his dark eyes searching. Renzo Valenti.

The father of this baby. The man who had so callously sent her away three days earlier. She hadn't expected to see him again. Not when he had been so adamant about the fact that he would have nothing to do with the child. That he didn't even believe her story.

But here he was.

A surge of hope went through her. Hope for the child. And—she had to confess internally, with no small amount of guilt—hope for her. Hope that she would be compensated for the surrogacy, as she had been promised.

She wiped her hands on her apron, stuffing a bar towel in the front pocket and striding across the room. She waved a hand, and the quick movement must have caught his attention, because just then, his gaze locked on to hers.

And everything slowed.

Something happened to her. A rush of heat flowed down through her body, pooling in her stomach, and slightly lower. Suddenly, her breasts felt heavy, her breath coming in short, harsh bursts. She was immobilized by that stare. By the fathomless, black depths that seemed to pin her there, like a butterfly in one of the collections her brothers had had.

She was trembling. And she had no idea why. Very few things intimidated her. Since she had stood there in front of her father—in front of the whole commune, like a bad movie or something—refusing to recant the "evil" things she had brought in from the outside, there wasn't much that bothered her. She had clung to what she wanted, defying everything she had been taught, defying her father, leading to her expulsion from the only home she'd ever known. That moment made everything else seem mundane in many ways.

Perhaps, she had imagined, the world would turn out to be every bit as scary and dangerous as her mother and father had promised her it would be. But once she had purposed in herself that she was willing to take that chance to discover herself, to discover her freedom, she had made peace with it. With whatever might happen.

But she was shaking now. Was intimidated. Was maybe even a little bit afraid.

And then he began to close the space between them. And it felt as though there was a connection between the two of them. As though there was a string tied around her waist, one he was holding in his hands. And even though he was the one drawing nearer to her, she felt the pull to him.

It was loud in the bar, but when he spoke it cut through like a knife. Effortless, sharp and exceedingly clear. "I think you and I need to have a little chat."

"We tried that," she said, shocked at how foreign her voice sounded. How breathless. "It didn't exactly go like I planned on it going."

"Well, you walked into my home and dropped a bombshell on me. So, I'm not entirely certain how you expected it to go."

"Well, I didn't know it was a bombshell. I thought we were just going to discuss something you already knew. A bombshell you were complicit in."

"Sadly for you, I was not complicit. But if what you're saying is true, we definitely need to come to an agreement of some kind."

"What I'm saying is absolutely true. I have the documentation back at the hostel."

He narrowed his eyes. "And I'm supposed to believe that this documentation is factual?"

She laughed. "I wouldn't know where to begin forging medical paperwork like that."

"That means nothing to me. Your word means nothing to me. I don't know who you are. I don't know anything about you. All I know is that you showed up at my house earlier and are now asking me to believe the most fantastical of tales. Why should I?"

"Well," she said, looking down at her sandaled feet, "I suppose because you're here." She looked back up at him, her breath catching in her throat when she met with his furious gaze. "That means you must think it could be true. And if it could be true, why wouldn't it be? Why would I target you? Why would I…I don't know. It's just… Trust me. I would never have cooked this up on my own."

"Take me back to your hostel."

"I'm just off shift. I need to go write down my time."

He reached out, grabbing hold of her bare arm. The contact between his fingers and her skin sent an electric crackle down through her body. She had to think. Really think if she had ever been touched like this by a man. Other than a doctor or her family members, she'd had very little physical contact with anyone. And this seemed… It seemed more than significant. It burned her all the way down to the soles of her feet. Made her feel like her shoes might melt.

Like *she* might melt.

"I will speak to your boss later if need be. But you're coming with me now."

"I shouldn't."

A smile curved his lips. It was not kind. It did nothing to dispel any of the tension in her chest. If anything, it made everything feel heavier. Tighter. "But you will, *cara mia*. You will."

After that statement of declaration, she found herself being propelled out of the open-air bar and onto the busy street. It was still teeming with people, humidity hanging in the overly warm air. Her hair was sticking to the back of her neck, her tank top sticking to her skin, and his body was like a furnace beside her as they strode purposefully down the street.

"You don't know where I live."

"Yes I do. I am fully capable of looking up the name of a hostel and finding the directions. And I know the streets well."

"This isn't the way back," she said, feeling the need to try to find some power in the situation. She despised feeling helpless. Despised feeling controlled.

"Yes," he said, "it is."

Much to her dismay, this alternate route seemed to put them back at the front door of the hostel much more quickly than the one she typically took. She pursed her lips together, frowning deeply.

"You're welcome," he said, pushing the door open, his entire posture and tone radiating a kind of arrogance she had never before come into contact with.

"For what?"

"I have just showed you a better route home. Likely I will save you time in the future. You're welcome."

She scowled, ducking her head and walking past him into the narrow hallway. She led him down the hall, to the small room that she had in the back. There were four bunk beds in it, with two other women currently occupying the space. It was fairly private, all things considered. Though, as Esther began to feel more symptomatic of her pregnancy, it began to feel more and more crowded.

She kicked her sandals off, making her way across the pale, uneven stone floor, and headed to the bottom bunk, where all of her things were kept when she wasn't sleeping. Her backpack was shoved into the corner by the wall, and she grabbed hold of it, dragging it toward her.

When she didn't hear footsteps following her, she turned to see Renzo standing in the doorway. His frame filled the space, and when he took that first step inside, he seemed to bring something with him. Tension. A presence that filled not only the room, but any empty space in her chest.

"Welcome," she said, her tone flat.

"Thank you," he responded, his words carrying a level of disdain that was almost comical. Except, it was difficult to find much of anything funny at the moment.

She tugged on the drawstring that kept her backpack cinched shut, then hunted around for the tightly folded papers that were down in the bottom. "This is it." She held it out to him and he took it. His fingertips didn't brush hers, and she found herself preoccupied by the realization that she had almost hoped they would.

"What is all of this?" he asked, unfolding the documents.

"Medical records of everything and the signed agreement. With both mine and Ashley's signature. I suppose you would know if it looked different from your wife's actual signature. And I think we can both agree that the likelihood of me randomly being able to forge it is slim."

He frowned, deep lines forming between his dark brows. "This seems… It seems like perhaps there could be some truth."

"Call Ashley. Call her. She's mad at me. I'm sure she'll be more than happy to yell at you, too."

"Ashley wants you to end the pregnancy?"

Esther nodded, swallowing hard. "I can't. I agreed to

this. And even though the baby isn't mine, without me, maybe it wouldn't exist. And I just… I can't."

"Well, if this is in fact my child, that isn't what I want either."

"You want the baby?"

She tried to read his expression, but she found it impossible. Not that she was exceptionally adept at decoding what people were thinking. She had spent so many years growing up in a closed community. Seeing any faces at all that were unfamiliar was a shock. Going out into the wide world after an entire life being cloistered was… There were so many sights. So many sounds and smells. Different voices, different accents. Different ways of expressing happiness, sadness.

While she often felt at a disadvantage, sometimes she wondered if she actually read people a bit better than those who didn't have to look as closely at the people around them. She always felt that if she released hold on her vigilance—even for a second—she would find herself lost in this endless sea of humanity.

But there were no clues at all on Renzo's face. It was as though he were carved from granite. His lips pressed into a firm line, his black eyes flat. Endless.

"I will take responsibility for my child," he said, which was not the same as wanting the child. But she supposed, it didn't matter.

"Well…I suppose that's…" She didn't want to ask about payment. Except, she desperately wanted to ask about payment.

"But the first thing we must do is get you out of this…" He looked around the room, his lip curling slightly. "This place. You cannot stay here. Not while you are carrying the heir to the Valenti fortune."

She blinked rapidly. The baby that she was carrying

was the heir to a fortune? She knew that Renzo was rich. Of course she did. She had seen the way that Ashley was accustomed to living after their stay at the lavish hotel the other woman had insisted they stay in when they'd gone across the border for the procedure.

Still. This revelation seemed different. "But we've been fine for the past couple of months," she said.

"Perhaps. Though, I imagine our definition of 'fine' may be sharply different from one another's. You are not to work at that bar, not anymore. And you will come with me. Back to my villa."

Esther felt like she had been punched in the chest. She found that she couldn't breathe. She felt immobilized. Utterly and completely weighted down by that dark, uncompromising gaze.

"But what if I... What if I don't want to?"

"You don't have a choice," he returned. "There is a clause in this agreement that says Ashley can choose to terminate it should she decide she no longer wants the pregnancy carried to term. That has happened. That means unless you comply with my demands, with my word, you will get nothing. And you will have no recourse. Not—I assure you—in Italy. I will pay you more than the sum my wife agreed on, but only if you do exactly as I say."

Her head was spinning. She felt like she needed to sit down or she was going to fall down. She found herself doing exactly that before she even realized it, her weak legs folding, plopping her down roughly onto the edge of the thin mattress, the wood frame digging sharply into her thighs.

The noise from outside filtered through the single-pane windows, joining the thoughts in her head, swirling around, making her feel dizzy. "Okay," she said, only because she could think of no discernible reason to refuse him.

She knew there were other consequences to consider. Concerns for her safety, perhaps? She didn't know him. Didn't know him in any way beyond a brief understanding of his reputation as a businessman.

She also knew that he had been married to Ashley. Ashley, who had proved to be untrustworthy. Manipulative and—if Renzo was to be believed—a liar.

So, she imagined that said something about his character.

But she didn't see another option. Not one beyond putting herself through something that would undoubtedly be both physically and emotionally demanding without any kind of recourse. Not for the first time, she felt a deep sense of guilt and regret.

She tried not to traffic too much in guilt. Mostly because she had spent so much of her life neck deep in it. Every time she found a book at the local book exchange and slipped it into her bag—one she knew she shouldn't have. Every time she figured out a way to smuggle in a CD she shouldn't have had.

When she'd been kicked out after the discovery of her smuggled items, she'd become determined to live life on her own terms. To shamelessly adore pop music, and sugared cereal and movies. To read all the books she wanted, including books with dirty words and dirty scenes. And to feel not even a hint of shame.

But on this score, it was difficult for her to feel anything but a creeping sense of shame. She had seized this opportunity because it had seemed like a chance for her to make her dreams come true. To go to school. To continue to travel. To start a life that would remain completely separate from where she had come from.

She had been so single-minded, so focused, so determined to keep herself from ever returning to her family, to that small, claustrophobic existence, that she had ignored any and all twinges of discomfort over this arrangement.

But now, it was impossible to ignore. Impossible to wave her hand over the fact that she was carrying a baby. That she had some kind of responsibility in all of this. That it would be incredibly hard on her body. That it would likely wreck her emotionally. And that if she didn't comply with what Renzo was asking her to do...

There was a very good chance she would come out of it diminished. That the strength she had gained, strength enough to strike out on her own, would be gone. And for what? For money she wouldn't even be able to get.

So, she found herself cinching her backpack back up. Slipping her feet into her sandals, and turning to face Renzo.

"Okay," she said, her lips feeling slightly numb. "I'm going with you."

# CHAPTER THREE

ADRENALINE AND ANGER coursed through Renzo in equal measure on the car ride back to his villa. It did not escape him that the woman—whose name he had read in the documents, but whom he had yet to be formally introduced to—was looking around the Italian-made vehicle with an expression akin to a country mouse. But he found he could spare little thought to it.

Not when the reality of the situation was so sharp. When his pulse was beating a steady tattoo in his throat, when his blood was running hot and fast beneath his skin. A baby. Esther Abbott, this American backpacker, was pregnant with his baby. Yes, he would have to verify all of this with Ashley, but he was forced to believe Esther. Though he had no real reason to.

Nothing beyond gut instinct. The idea of trusting his gut nearly made him laugh. But then, he rarely trusted his gut. Usually, he trusted in parts lower. And his own quick intellect, which he often allowed himself to imagine was above reproach.

In matters of business, it was. When he was consulted on where a certain business should be built, when he was tasked with seeing to a major bit of real estate development, he never failed. Instincts, inherited from his father, drove him in that arena.

Apparently, in other matters he was not quite so discerning. Or so unerring. His ex-wife was one of the very prominent examples of that truth.

Jillian being another.

Women. It seemed he had a tendency to be a fool for women. No matter that he kept his heart out of any such entanglements, he seemed to have a knack for finding women who got him in other ways.

He looked sideways at Esther, then quickly turned his focus back to the road. He would have no such issues with her. She was plain. Pretty, he supposed. But her wide brown eyes were unlined, unenhanced in any way. Her dark eyebrows a bit heavier than he typically liked on a woman. There were vague bruised-looking circles beneath her eyes, and he couldn't work out if that was because of exhaustion, or if it was simply part of her coloring.

He was so accustomed to seeing women with a full face of makeup that was near enough to airbrushing in real life that he found it very hard to say.

Her lips were full, dusky, and he thought probably the most attractive thing about her. Though, her body was also nice enough. Her breasts weren't large, but they were beautiful shaped, and it was clear she wasn't wearing a bra beneath that black tank top of hers.

But her breasts were immaterial. The only thing that mattered was her womb. And whether or not his child currently resided inside it.

He turned sharply into his driveway, leaving the gate wide open, and not particularly caring. Then, he got out of the car, rounding it and jerking open the passenger door. "Welcome to your new home," he said, knowing that his tone sounded anything but welcoming.

She bit her bottom lip, gathering her backpack from the floor of the car, and getting out, holding the offensive canvas bag to her chest. She looked around, eyes wide, a sort of sickly pallor appearing beneath her tan skin.

"You were just here a couple of days ago," he said. "You can stop looking so intimidated."

"Well," she said, directing her focus to him, "you're intimidating. A house like this... One that is practically a castle... That's intimidating." She took a deep breath. "And I know I was here earlier. But this is different. I was focused on telling you about the baby. I wasn't thinking I would stay here."

"Are you going to pretend that you would prefer the hostel? There is no need to pretend with me. You agreed to carry a child for money. It isn't as though you can suddenly make believe you have no interest in material things."

She shook her head. "I don't. I mean, not the way that you think. I want to go to college."

He frowned. "How old are you?"

"Twenty-three."

He held back a curse. She was the same age as his sister, Allegra. Possibly a bit younger. Had he been the sort of man who possessed the ability to feel sympathy for strangers, he thought he might feel some for her. But those softer feelings had been bled from him long ago, empathy replaced by a vague sense of concern.

"And you couldn't access any scholarships?"

"No. I had to pay to take the SATs. I didn't exactly go to high school. But my scores are good enough to get into a few places. I think. I just need to get my financial ducks in a row."

"You didn't go to high school?"

She pursed her lips together. "I was homeschooled. Kind of. Anyway, it isn't like I was trying to get myself a yacht. And even if I was, nobody does surrogacy for free for a stranger."

He lifted a shoulder. "I suppose not. Come this way."

He led the way into the villa, suddenly completely at a loss. His housekeeper had already retired to her quarters, and here he was with an urchin whom he suddenly had to manage. "I imagine you're tired," he said.

"Hungry," she replied.

He gritted his teeth. "The kitchen is this way."

He led her through the expensive house, listening to the sound of her shuffling footsteps behind him as they made their way to the kitchen. The house itself was old. Stonework dating back centuries. But inside, all of the modern conveniences had been supplied. He made his way to the large stainless steel fridge and opened it. "You may have your pick of what's inside."

As soon as he said that, he realized that most of the food was still ingredients, and not exactly a meal. But surely, there would be something. Then he remembered that his housekeeper often left portions in the freezer for him just in case.

He didn't often eat at home, and he would just as soon go out if there was no staff on hand to make him something. But he was not going back out tonight.

He looked until he found what looked to be a container of pasta. "Here you go," he said, setting it down in front of a wide-eyed Esther.

He didn't stay to see what she did after that. Instead, he strode from the room, taking the stairs two at a time and heading toward his office. He paced the length of the room for a moment, then turned to his desk, taking hold of his phone and dialing his ex-wife.

It took only two rings for Ashley to answer. That didn't surprise him. If she was going to answer, of course she would do it quickly. Otherwise, had she intended to ignore

him, she would have done so steadfastly. She was nothing if not extreme.

"Renzo," she said, sounding bored. "To what do I owe
the pleasure?"

"You may not find it such a pleasure to speak to me,
Ashley. Not when you hear what I have to say."

"I have not actually found it a pleasure to speak to you
for quite a few months."

"We were only married for six months, so I hope that's
an exaggeration."

"It isn't. Why do you think I had to find other men to
satisfy me?"

"If you are talking about emotional satisfaction, I have
several answers for that. However, if you mean to imply
that I did not satisfy you physically, then I'm going to have
to call you a liar."

Ashley huffed. "There's more to life than sex."

"Yes indeed. There is, in fact, the small matter of the
woman who is currently downstairs in my kitchen."

"We're divorced now," Ashley said, her voice so sharp
it could cut glass. "Who is or is not in your kitchen—or
bed—is none of my concern."

"It is when it's Esther Abbott. A woman who claims that
she had an agreement with you. For her to carry *our* child."

There was a pause. He was almost satisfied that he
had clearly succeeded in rendering Ashley speechless. It
was such a difficult thing to do. Even when she had been
caught in bed with someone else, she had done her best
to talk, scream and cry her way out of it. She was not one
to let it rest. She was never one to let someone else have
the last word.

Her silence now was telling. Though, of her absolute surprise, or of her chagrin at being found out, he didn't know.

"I thought it might save us. But that was before…

Before the divorce was final. Before you found out about the others."

"Right. The five other men that you were with during the course of our marriage?"

Ashley laughed. "Seven, I think."

It didn't matter to him. Five, seven or only the one he had actually witnessed. He had a feeling the truth didn't matter to Ashley either. It was all about scoring points.

"So this is true," he said, his tone harsh.

"Yes," she replied, her voice tight.

"How?" he bit out.

She huffed out an impatient-sounding laugh. "Well, darling, the last time we were intimate you used a condom. I just…made use of it after you discarded it. It was enough for the doctor."

He swore. At her. At himself. At his body. "Is there nothing too low for you?"

"I guess that remains to be seen," she said, her tone brittle like glass. "I have a lot of living left to do, but don't worry, Renzo, you won't be part of it. My depths will not be of any concern to you."

"This woman is pregnant with *our* child," he said, trying to bring it back around to the topic at hand. To the reason he had some creature-ish backpacker in his home.

"Because she is stubborn. I told her she didn't have to continue with it. In fact, I told her I refused to pay the remainder of the fee."

"Yes," he bit out. "I have had a discussion with her. I was only calling you to confirm."

"What are you going to do?"

That was a good question. An excellent question. He was going to raise the child, naturally. But how was he going to explain it? To his parents. To the media. These would be headlines his child would read. Either he would have to be honest about Ashley's deception, or he would have to concoct a story about a mother abandoning her child.

That would not do.

But surrogacy was not legal in Italy. No agreement would be binding within these borders. And he would use that to his advantage.

"There is nothing to be done," he said, his tone swift, decisive. "Esther Abbott is pregnant with my child. And I will do the responsible thing."

"Renzo," she said, her voice fierce, "what do you intend to do?"

He knew. There was no question. He had been in a situation similar to this before. Only then, he had had no power. The woman involved, her husband, his parents, had all made the decisions around him. His ill-advised affair with Jillian costing much more than his virginity.

At sixteen, he had become a father for the first time. But he had been barred from having anything to do with the child. A story carefully constructed to protect her marriage, her family, that child and his reputation had been agreed on by all.

All except for Renzo.

He would not allow such a thing to happen again. He would not allow himself to be sidelined. He would not put him, or his child, in such a precarious position. There was only one thing to do. And he would see it done.

"I shall do what any responsible man would do in this situation. I intend to marry Esther Abbott."

Esther had never seen anything quite like Renzo's kitchen. It had taken her more than ten minutes to figure out how to use the microwave. And even then, the pasta had ended up having cold spots and spots that scalded her tongue. Still, it was one of the best things she had ever tasted.

That probably had more to do with exhaustion and how long she'd gone without eating than anything else. Pasta was one of her favorite newly discovered foods, though. Not that she'd never had noodles in some form. It was just that her mother typically made them for soups, and not the way she'd had it served in Italy.

Discovering new foods had been her favorite part of travel so far. Scones in England with clotted cream, macarons in France. She had greatly enjoyed the culinary adventure, nearly as much as the rest of it.

Though, sometimes she missed brown bread and stew. The kinds of simple foods her mother made from scratch at home.

A swift kick of loneliness, of homesickness, punched her low in the stomach. It was unusual, but it did happen sometimes. Most of her home life had been difficult. Had been nothing at all like the way she wanted to live. But it had been safe. And for most of her life, it had been the only thing she'd known.

She blinked, taking another bite of her pasta, and allowing the present moment to wash away the slow-burning ache of nostalgia.

She heard footsteps and looked up. Renzo strode into the kitchen, and that dark black gaze burned away the remaining bit of homesickness. There was no room for anything inside her, nothing beyond that sharp, cutting intensity.

"I just spoke to Ashley."

Suddenly, the pasta felt like sawdust in Esther's mouth. "I imagine she told you the thing you didn't want to hear."

"You are correct in your assessment."

"I'm sorry. But it's true. I really didn't come here to take advantage of you, or to lie to you. And I really couldn't have forged any kind of medical documents. I had never even been to a doctor until Ashley took me for the procedure."

He frowned. She could tell that she had said something that had revealed her as being different. She did that a lot. Mostly because she didn't exactly know the line. Cultures were different, after all, and sometimes she thought people might assume she was different only because she was American.

But she was different from typical Americans, too.

"I lived in a small town," she said, the lie rolling off her tongue easily. She had always been a liar. Because if ever her parents asked her if she was content, if ever her mother had asked her about her plans for the future, she'd had to lie.

And so, covering up the extent of just how strange she was became easier and easier as she talked to more people and picked up more of what was expected.

"A town so small you did not have doctors?"

"He made house calls." That part was true. There had been a physician in the commune.

"Regardless of your past history, it seems that you were telling the truth."

"I said I was."

"Yes, you did. It is an unenviable position you find yourself in—or perhaps it is enviable, depending on your perspective. Tell me, Esther, what are your goals in life?"

It was a strange question. And never once had she been asked. Not really. Her parents had spoken to her about what she would do. About what her duty was, about the purposes of women and what they had to do to be fulfilled. But no one had ever asked her if it would fulfill her. No one had ever asked her anything at all.

But he was asking. And that made something warm glow inside her.

It made her want to tell him.

"I want to travel. And I want to go to school. I want to get an education."

"To what end?" he asked.

"What do you mean?"

"What do you wish to major in? Business? History? Art?"

"Everything." She shrugged. "I just want to know things."

"What do you want to know?"

"Everything I didn't before."

"That is an incredibly tall order. But one that is certainly possible. Is there a better city in the world to learn about history? Rome."

"Paris and London might have differing opinions. But I definitely take your point. And yes, I agree I can get quite an education here simply by being here. But I want more."

He began to pace, and there was something in that stride, attention, a purpose, that made her feel a bit like a small, twitchy little field mouse standing in front of a big cat. "Why shouldn't you have more? Why shouldn't you have everything? Look around you," he said, sweeping his hand in a broad gesture. "I am a man in possession of most everything. For what reason? Simply because I was born into it. And yes, I have done all that I can to ensure I am worthy of the position. I assumed the helm of the family business and have continued to navigate it with proficiency."

"That's very nice for you," she said, mostly because she had no idea what else she was supposed to say.

"It could be very nice for you," he said, leveling his eyes on her. Her skin prickled, somewhere beneath the surface, where she couldn't tamp it down, not even by grabbing hold of her elbows and rubbing her forearms vigorously.

"Could it?"

"I am not going to be coy. I am a billionaire, Ms. Abbott. A man with a limitless supply of resources. Ashley was not as generous with you as she might have been. But I intend to give you the world."

She felt her face growing warm. She cleared her throat, reaching up and tucking a strand of hair behind her ear, just so she had something to do with the reckless energy surging through her. "That's very nice. But I only have the one backpack. I'm not sure the world would fit inside it."

"That is the catch," he said.

"What is?"

"You will have to give up the backpack."

She blinked. "I'm not sure I understand."

"I am a man with a great deal of power—that, I should think, is obvious. However, there are a few things I am bound by. Public perception is one of them. The extremely conservative ideals of my parents are another. My parents have gone to great lengths in my life to ensure that I became the man that I am today." His jaw seemed to tighten when he said that, a muscle there twitching slightly. "And while I was certainly pushing the edges of propriety by marrying Ashley, I did marry her. Marriage, children, that is what is expected of me. What is not expected? To have a surrogacy scandal. To have it leak out to the public that my wife conspired against me. I will not be made a fool of, Esther," he said, using her first name for the first time. "I will not have the Valenti name made foolish by my mistake."

"I don't understand what that has to do with me. You're going to have to be very direct, because sometimes I'm a little bit slow with shorthand."

He frowned. "Just how small is that town you're from?"

"Very small. Very, very small."

"Perhaps the size of the town makes no difference. Admittedly, we are in a bit of an unprecedented situation. Still, my course is clear."

"Please do enlighten me."

He paused, looking at her. Which shouldn't have been significant. He had looked at her before. Lots of times. People looked at each other when they talked. Except, this time when he looked at her it felt different.

But this was different. Whether or not that made any sense, it was different. His gaze was assessing now, in a different way from what it had been before. As though he were looking deeper. Beneath her clothes, the thought of which made her feel hot all over, down beneath her skin. As though he were trying to see exactly what her substance was.

He looked over her entire body, and she felt herself begin to burn everywhere his gaze made contact. That strange, restless feeling was back between her thighs, an intense heaviness in her breasts.

She sucked in a sharp breath, trying to combat the sting of tears that were beginning to burn there. She didn't know why she wanted to cry. Except that this felt big, new and completely unfamiliar. Whatever this was.

"Esther Abbott," he said, his words sliding over her name like silk, "you are going to be my wife."

# CHAPTER FOUR

ESTHER FELT LIKE she was dreaming. She had a strange sense of being detached from her body, of looking down on the scene below her, like it was happening to somebody else and not her. Because there was no way she was standing in the middle of a historic mansion, looking at the most beautiful man she had ever seen in her entire life, his proposal still ringing in her ears.

*Beautiful* was the wrong word for Renzo, she decided. He was too hard cut. His cheekbones sharp, his jaw like a blade. His dark eyes weren't any softer. Just like the rest of him, they were enticing, but deadly. Like broken edges of obsidian. So tempting to run your fingers over the seemingly smooth surface, until you caught an edge and sliced into your own flesh.

It struck her just how ridiculous it was, fixating on her mental use of the word *beautiful*. Fixating on his appearance at all. He had just stated his intention to make her his wife. *His wife.*

That was her worst nightmare. Being owned by a man again. She couldn't stand it. Never. Yes, Renzo was different from her father. Certainly this was a different situation. But it felt the same. It made her feel like her throat was closing up, like the walls were closing in around her.

"No," she said, panic a clawing beast scurrying inside

her. "That's impossible. I can't do that. I have goals. Goals that do not include being your... No."

"There is not a single goal that you possess that I cannot enable you to meet with greater ease and better style."

She shook her head. "But don't you see? That isn't the point. I don't want to stay here in Rome. I want to see the world."

"You have been seeing the world, have you not? Hostels, and dirty bars. How very romantic. I imagine it is difficult to do much sightseeing when you are tethered to whatever table you are waiting at any given time."

"I have time off. I'm living in the city. I have what I want. Maybe you don't understand, but as you said, you had very much of what you possess given to you. Inherited. My legacy is nothing. A tiny little house with absolutely no frills in the middle of the mountain range. And that's not even mine. It's just my father's. And it never would've passed to me. It would've gone to one of my six brothers. Yes, *six* brothers. But not to any of my three sisters. You heard that number right, too. Because there was nothing for us. Nothing at all for women. Though, I'm not entirely certain that in that scenario the boys have it much better." She took a deep breath. "I'm proud of this. Of what I have. I'm not going to allow you to make me feel like it's lacking."

"But it is lacking, *cara*." The words cut her like a knife. "If it were not lacking, you would not have goals to transcend it. You wish to go to school. You wish to learn things. You wish to see the world. Come into my world. I guarantee you it is much more expansive than any that you might hope to enter on your own."

The words reverberated through her, an echo. A promise. One that almost every fiber of her being wanted to run from. Almost. There must have been some part of her that was intrigued. That wanted to stay. Because there she was, as rooted to the spot as she had been when he entered the bar earlier that night. There was something about him that did that to her, and it seemed to be more powerful than every terrified, screaming cell in her brain that told her she should run.

"That's insanity. I don't need you, I just need the payment that was agreed upon, and then I can better my circumstances."

"But why have a portion of my fortune when you can have access to the entire thing?"

"I wouldn't have the first idea what to do with that. Frankly, having anything to call mine is something of a new experience. What you're talking about seems a little bit beyond my scope."

"Ah, but it does not have to be." His words were like velvet, his voice wrapping itself around her. Her mother had been right. The devil wasn't ugly. That wouldn't work when it came to doling out temptation. The devil was beautiful. The devil—she was becoming more and more certain—was Renzo Valenti.

"I think you might be crazy. I think that I understand now why your wife left you."

He chuckled. "Is that what she told you? One of her many lies. I was the one who threw that grasping, greedy shrew out onto the streets, after I caught her in bed with another man."

Esther tried not to look shocked. She tried not to look as innocent and gauche as she was. The idea that somebody would violate their marriage vows so easily was foreign to her. Marriage was sacred, in her upbringing. Another reason that what Renzo was suggesting was completely beyond the pale for her.

"She cheated on you?"

"Yes, she did. As I said to you earlier, I, for my part, was faithful to my wife. I will not lie and say that I chose Ashley out of any deep love for her, but initially our connection was fun at least."

Esther turned that over for a moment. "Fun?"

"In some rooms, yes."

The exact meaning of what he was saying slipped past her slightly, but she knew that he was implying something lascivious, and it made her face get hot. "Well, that is…I don't…I'm not the wife for you," she finished. Because if she couldn't exactly form a picture to go with what he was trying to imply here, she knew—beyond a shadow of a doubt—that she could never be in that kind of relationship with him.

She had never even been kissed. Being a wife… Well, she had no experience in that area. Not only that, she had no desire to be. Oh, probably eventually she would want to be with someone. It was on the list. Way far down.

Sex was a curiosity to her. She'd read love scenes in books, seen them in movies. But she knew she wasn't ready for it herself, not so much because of the physical part, but the connecting-to-another-person part.

And for now, she was too busy exploring who she was. What she wanted from life. She had never seen a marriage where the man was not unquestionably in control. Had no experience of male and female relationships where the husband did not rule the wife with an iron fist.

She would never subject herself to that. Never.

"Why is that? Because you harbor some kind of childish fantasy of marrying for love?"

"No. Not at all. I harbor fantasies of never marrying, actually. And as for love? I have never seen it. Not the way that you're talking about it. What I have seen is possession and control. And I have no interest in that."

"I see. So, you are everything that you appear to be. Someone who changes with the wind and moves at will."

He spoke with such disdain, and it rankled. "Yes. And I never pretended to be anything else. Why should I? I don't have any obligation to you. I don't have any obligation to anyone, and that's how I like it. But I got myself into this situation, and I do intend to act with integrity. At least, as I see it. I wanted to make sure you knew about the baby, I wanted to make sure that your wishes were being met."

"And yet, you saw no point in checking in with me in the first place?"

She let out a long, slow breath. "I know. I should have. But that was part of why I came to find you after Ashley said she no longer wanted the baby. Because she had made it so clear that you wanted a child desperately in the first place, and I could not believe that you would suddenly change your mind. Not based on everything she had said."

"A convincing liar, is my ex-wife."

"Clearly. But I don't want to be tangled up in any of this. I just want to have the baby and go on my way."

"That… That can be discussed. But for all intents and purposes, we are going to present you to the world as my lover. What happens after the birth of the child can be negotiated, but we will conduct ourselves as an engaged couple until then."

"I don't understand… I don't want…"

"I am a very powerful man. The fact that I'm not throwing you over my shoulder and carrying you off to the nearest church, where I have no doubt I could bring the clergy around to my way of thinking, shows that I'm being somewhat magnanimous with you. I am also not overly enticed to jump back into marriage, not after what I have just been through. So, it is decided. You will play the part of my fiancée, at least until the birth of the child, at which point your freedom—and the parting price—can be negotiated."

"We will be in the news?" The idea of her parents seeing her with him… It terrified her.

"Tabloids most likely. Perhaps some lifestyle sections of respectable papers. But that will mostly be contained to Europe."

She let out a slow breath, releasing some of the tension that had built in her chest. "Okay. Maybe that isn't so bad."

He frowned. "Are you hiding from someone? Because I need to know. I need to know what might put my child in danger, *cara*."

"I'm not hiding from anyone. And, trust me, I'm not in danger. I mean, I'm kind of hiding. But not because I'm afraid somebody will come after me. My parents were… strict. And they don't approve of what I'm doing. I just don't want them to see me written about in the paper, with a man. Pregnant. Not married." In spite of the fact that she had long since given up hope of pleasing her parents—in fact, she had come to terms with the fact that her leaving home would mean cutting ties with them forever—she felt sick shame settle in her stomach.

"They are traditional then."

"You have no idea." The shame lingered, wouldn't leave. "They never even wanted me to wear makeup or anything."

"Well, I fear you will be defying that rule, as well."

"Why?" She had the freedom to wear whatever she wanted now, but she hadn't bought makeup yet. There had not been an occasion to.

"Because my women look a certain way."

That forced a very specific image into her head. A *certain* kind of woman. The kind of woman her mother often talked about. Fallen, scarlet.

She had a difficult time wrapping her head around the

idea that she would be presented to the world like that. Not because she felt ashamed, but because it just never occurred to her. The idea that she might be made up, and dressed up, on the arm of a man like Renzo Valenti.

"You go to... You go to a lot of events, don't you?"

"A great many. As I said to you before, the world that I will show you is far beyond anything you could access on your own. If you want to experience, I can give you experiences you didn't know to dream of."

Those words made something hot take root at the base of her spine, wrap around low and tight inside her, making her feel both hot and empty somehow.

"All right," she said, the words rushed, because they had to be. If she thought about it any longer, she would run away. "I'll do it."

"Do what exactly?" he said, his eyes hard on hers.

"I will play the part of your fiancée for as long as you want me to. And then after that... After the baby is born... I go."

He took a step forward, reaching out and taking hold of her chin between his thumb and forefinger. His touch burned. Caught hold of her like a wildfire and raged straight through her body. "Excellent. Esther," he said, her name like a caress on his lips, "you have yourself a fiancé."

Renzo knew that he was going to have to tread extremely carefully over the next few weeks. That was one of the few things he knew. Everything else in his life was upended. He had a disheveled little street urchin staying in one of his spare rooms, and he had to present her to the world as his chosen bride soon. Very soon. The sooner the better. Before Ashley got a chance to drop any poison into the ear of the media.

He had already set a plan in motion to ensure she would

not. A very generous payout that his lawyer would be offering to hers by the time the sun rose in Canada. She would not want to defy him. Not when—without this—she would be getting nothing from him due to the ironclad prenuptial agreement they had entered into before the marriage.

Ashley liked attention, that much was true. But she liked money even more. That would take care of her.

But then there was the small matter of his parents. And his parents were never actually a small matter.

He imagined that—regardless of the circumstances—they would be thrilled to learn that they were expecting a grandchild. Really, they would only be all the happier knowing that Ashley was out of the picture.

But Esther was most certainly a problem he would have to solve.

With great reluctance, he picked up his phone and dialed his mother's number. She picked up on the first ring. "Renzo. You don't call me enough."

"Yes, so I hear. Every time I call."

"And it is true every time. So, tell me, what is on your agenda? Because you never call just to make small talk."

He couldn't help but laugh at that. His mother knew him far too well. "Yes, as it happens, I was wondering if you had any plans for dinner."

"Why yes, Renzo. I in fact have dinner plans every day. Tonight, we are having lamb, vegetables and a risotto."

"Excellent, Mother. But do you have room at your table?"

"For?"

"Myself," he said, amused at his mother's obstinance. "And a date."

"Dating already. So soon after your divorce." His mother said that word as though it were anathema. But then, he supposed that was because for her it was.

"Yes, Mother. Actually, more than dating. I intend to introduce you to my fiancée, Esther Abbott."

The line went silent. That concerned him much more than a tirade of angry Italian ever could. Then, his mother spoke. "Abbott? Who are her people?"

He thought of what she'd said about the mountain cabin her rather larger-than-usual family lived in, and he was tempted to laugh. "No one you would know."

"Please tell me you have not chosen another Canadian, Renzo."

"No, on that score you can relax. She is an American."

The choking sound he heard on the other end of the line was not altogether unexpected. "That," she said finally, "is even worse."

"Even so, the decision is made." He considered telling her about the pregnancy over the phone, but decided that it was one of those things his mother would insist on hearing about in person. She did like to divide her news into priorities like that. She had never gotten over Allegra's pregnancy news filtering back to her through the gossip chain.

"So very typical of you." There was no real condemnation or venom in her tone. Though, the simple statement forced him to think back to a time when it had not been true. When he had allowed other people to force his hand when it came to decision making. He tried very hard not to think about Jillian. About the daughter who was being raised by another man. A daughter he sometimes caught glimpses of at various functions.

Just one of the many reasons he worked so hard to keep his alcohol intake healthy at such things. It was much better to remember very little of it the next day, he found.

He had been sixteen when his parents had encouraged him to make that decision. And since then, he had changed the way he operated. Completely, utterly. He was not bitter at his mother and father. They had pushed him into making the best decision they could see.

And hell, it had been the best decision. He had proved that fifty times over in the years since. He had not been ready to be a father. But he was ready now.

"Yes, I am typical as ever. But will we be welcome at your table tonight, or not?"

"It will be an ordeal. We will have to purchase more ingredients."

"When you say 'we,' you mean your staff, whom you pay handsomely. I imagine it can all be arranged?"

"Of course it will be. You will be there at eight. Do not be late. Because I will not wait, and the one thing you do not want, Renzo, is for me to be one glass of wine ahead of you."

He felt his mouth turn upward. "That," he said, "is very true, Mother, I have no doubt."

He disconnected the call. Then, he made another call to the personal stylist his mother had used for years, asking that she clear her schedule and bring along a team of hair and makeup artists.

He was not sure if Esther had enough raw material to be salvageable. It was very difficult to say. The women whom he involved himself with tended to be either classic, polished pieces of architecture, or new constructions, as it were. He had no experience with full renovations.

Still, she was not unattractive. So, it seemed as though he should be able to fashion her into something that looked believable. The thought nearly made him laugh. She was pregnant. She was pregnant with his child. And while it may take a paternity test on his end to prove that to the world—or his parents—they would never ask for a test to prove maternity.

Therefore, by that very logic, people would believe their connection. But he would like to make it slightly easier.

When he went downstairs and found her sitting in the dining area, on the floor by the floor-to-ceiling windows, her face tilted up toward the sun, a bowl of cereal clutched tightly in her hands, he knew that he had made the right decision in bringing in an entire team.

"What are you doing?"

She squeaked, startling and sloshing a bit of milk over the edge of her bowl, onto the tile floor. "I was enjoying the morning," she said.

"There is a table for you to sit at." He gestured to the long, banquet-style piece of furniture, which had been carved from solid wood and was older than either of them, and was certainly more than good enough for this little hippie to sit and eat her cereal at.

"I know. But I wanted to sit by the window. And I could have moved a chair, but they're very heavy. And I didn't want to scuff the tile. And anyway, the floor is fine. It's warm from the sun."

"We are going to my parents' house for dinner tonight," he said, because it was as good a time as any to broach that subject. "And I trust you will not sit yourself on the floor then." The image of her crouched in a corner gnawing on a lamb shank was nearly comical. That would upset his mother. Though, seeing as she had been prewarned that Esther was an American, she might not find the behavior all that strange.

He regarded her for a moment. Her hair was caught up in that same messy bun she'd had it in yesterday, and she had traded her black tank top for a brown one, and yesterday's long, flowing skirt for one in a brighter color.

She frowned, her dark brows locking together. "Of course not." He had thought her face plain yesterday, and now, for some reason, he thought of it as freshly scrubbed. Clean. There was something… Not wholesome, for this exotic creature could never be called something so mundane, but something natural. Organic. As if she had materialized in a garden somewhere rather than being born.

Which was a much more fanciful thought than he had ever had about a woman before. Typically, his thoughts were limited to whether or not he thought they would look good naked, whether or not they would like to get naked with him, and then, after they had, how he might get rid of them.

"Good. My parents are not flexible people. Neither are they overly friendly. They are extremely old, Italian money. They are very proud of their lineage, and of our name. I told them that we are getting married. And that you're American. They are amused by neither. Or rather, my mother is amused by neither, and my father will follow suit."

Her dark eyes went round, the expression on her face worried. It was comical to him that she might be concerned over what his parents thought. Someone like her didn't seem as though she would concern herself with what other people thought.

"That doesn't sound like a very pleasant evening," she said, after a long pause.

"Oh, evenings with my parents are never what I would call pleasant. However, they are not fatal."

"I have an aversion to being judged," she said, her tone stiff.

"Oh, I quite enjoy it. I find it very liberating to lower people's expectations."

"You do not," she said, "nobody does. Everybody cares about pleasing their parents." She frowned. "Or, if not their parents, at least somebody."

"You said yourself, you left your parents. And that they weren't happy with you. Obviously, you don't worry overly much about pleasing your parents."

"But I did. For a long time. And the only reason I don't now is out of necessity. I mean, I would've never had any freedom if I hadn't let go of it."

There was a strange feeling in his chest, her words catching hold of something that seemed to tug on him, down deep.

About freedom. About letting go.

"Well, on that same subject, there is some work to be done if we are going to present you at dinner tonight."

"What sort of work?" She looked genuinely mystified at that statement, as though she had no idea what he might be referring to.

As he stood before her in his perfectly pressed custom suit, and she sat cross-legged on the floor looking like she would be more at home at a Renaissance fair than in his home, it occurred to him that she really was a strange creature. The differences between the two of them should be obvious, and yet, she did not seem to pick up on them on her own. Or rather, she didn't seem to care.

"You, Esther."

"What's wrong with me?"

"What did you plan on wearing to dinner tonight?"

She looked down. "This, I suppose."

"You do not see perhaps a small difference in the way that you are dressed, compared with the way that I am dressed?"

"Did you want me to wear a tux?"

"This is not a tux. It's a suit. There is a difference."

"Interesting. And good to know."

He had a feeling she did not find it interesting at all. "I have taken the liberty of having some clothing ordered for you." He lifted his hand and looked at his watch. "It should be here any moment."

Just then, his housekeeper came walking into the room, a concerned expression on her face. "Mr. Valenti, Tierra is here."

His stylist went by only one name. "Excellent."

"Should I have her meet you upstairs with all of her items?"

"Yes. But in Esther's room, if you don't mind."

Esther's eyes widened. "What exactly are you providing me with?"

"Something that doesn't look like it came out of the bottom of a bargain bin at some sort of rummage sale for mismatched fabrics."

She frowned. "Is that your way of saying there's something wrong with what I'm wearing?"

"No. My way of saying that is to say what you're wearing isn't suitable. Actually, it's perfectly suitable if you intend to continue to wait tables at a dusty bar crawling with tourists. However, it is not acceptable if you wish to be presented to the world as my fiancée, and neither is it acceptable for you to wear on the night you are to meet my parents."

At that, his housekeeper's face contorted. She began to speak at him in angry, rapid Italian that he was only grateful Esther likely wouldn't be able to decode. "She is pregnant with my child," he said. "There is nothing else to be done."

She shook her head. "You have become a bad man," she huffed, walking out of the room. That last part she had said in English.

"Why is she mad at you?"

"Well, likely because she thinks I impregnated some

poor American tourist while I was still married. You can see how she would find that upsetting."

"I suppose." She blinked. "But doesn't *she* work for *you*?"

"Luciana practically came with the house, which I purchased more than a decade ago. It's difficult to say sometimes who exactly works for whom."

She frowned. "And now what? You're going to…buy me new clothes?"

"Exactly. And take your old clothes and burn them."

"That isn't very nice."

He raised his brows, affecting his expression into one of mock surprise. "Is it not? That is regrettable. I do so strive to be nice."

"I doubt it."

"Don't snarl at me," he said. "And, remember, you have to pretend to be my fiancée. In front of Luciana, and in front of Tierra."

She scowled, but allowed him to direct her up the stairs, depositing her cereal bowl on the dining room table as she went. He watched the gentle sway of her hips as she began to ascend the staircase. When she was in motion, her clothing seemed less ridiculous. In fact, the effect was rather graceful.

There was an otherworldly quality to her that he couldn't quite pin down. Something that he had difficulty describing, even to himself. She was very young, and simultaneously sometimes seemed quite old. Like a being who had been dropped down to earth, knowing very little about the customs of those around her, and yet, somehow knowing more than any human could in a lifetime.

And that was fanciful thinking that he never normally allowed himself.

So instead of that, he focused on the rounded curve of her rear. Because that, at least, he understood.

When they reached the bedroom, the stylist had already unveiled a rack of clothing. She was fussing around with the hanging garments, smoothing pleats and adjusting the long, complicated skirts on the various gowns.

"Oh, my," she said, turning and getting her first look at Esther. "We do have our work cut out for us."

# CHAPTER FIVE

FOR THE NEXT two hours, Esther was pulled, prodded, poked with pins and clucked at. Well and truly clucked at. As though this woman, Renzo's stylist, was a chicken. And as though Esther was a naughty chick rather than a woman.

Renzo had left them to it, and she was thankful. Since the moment he had walked out, the other woman had begun stripping Esther's clothes off her body and forcing new undergarments, new dresses and new shoes onto her.

Esther had never felt fabrics like this. She had never seen styles like this on her spare curves. She had been all about experiencing new things since she had left her home, but she hadn't gotten around to the clothing and makeup. Or hair. That all required a disposable income that she simply didn't possess. She was more concerned with keeping food in her belly. And clothing herself in the basics, rather than exploring the world of fashion.

But now she felt as though she had been well and truly educated in which colors looked best on her, which shapes best suited her figure. Of course, most of it had happened in abrupt Italian that Esther could understand only parts of, but still. She could see herself.

In fact, right at the moment, she couldn't take her eyes off herself. She was wearing a dark green gown that had little cap sleeves and a plunging V neckline that showed off acres of skin around her neck and down farther. The kind of daring look that would never have been allowed in her family home.

The skirt was long, falling all the way down to the tops of the most beautiful pair of shoes Esther had ever seen. Of course, they were also the tallest pair of shoes she had ever worn, and she had serious doubts about her ability to walk in them.

Somewhere in the middle of the clothing frenzy, two men had arrived to work on her hair and makeup. And work they had. Her hair was tamed into a sleek, black curtain, a good half a foot cut off the near-unmanageable length.

Her eyes, which she had always thought were almost comically large, didn't look comical now. Though, they still looked large. They had been rimmed with black liner, the corners of her eyes highlighted with gold. They had brushed something onto her cheeks, too, making them glow. And her lips… A bit of pale, burnished orange gloss colored them, just slightly, highlighting them, just enough.

She looked like a stranger. She couldn't see so many of the defining features of her face, not the way she usually did. Those dark circles that had permanent residence beneath her eyes were diminished, her nose somehow appearing more narrow, her cheeks a bit more hollow, thanks to a technique they had called contouring.

And then there was her body. She had never thought much about it. She didn't have overly large breasts, and for convenience, she typically opted not to wear a bra, sticking to plain, high-necked tops in dark colors that she always hoped concealed enough.

Even though this gown still didn't allow for a bra, it created an entirely different effect on her bustline than the simple cotton tank tops she preferred. Her breasts looked rounder, fuller, her waist a bit more dramatically curved, rather than straight up and down. The shape of the skirt enhanced the appearance of her hips, making her look like she almost had an hourglass figure.

It was strange to see herself this way. With all her attributes enhanced, rather than downplayed.

The bedroom door opened and she froze when Renzo walked in. She felt hideously exposed in a way that she never had before. Because for the first time in her life she was aware that she might look beautiful, and that there was a man who was most certainly beautiful looking her over. Appraising her as he might a work of art.

"Well," he said, turning his focus to the team of people who had accomplished the effect, and away from her, "this is a very pleasant surprise."

"She is a dream to dress," Tierra said. "Everything fits so nicely. And that golden skin of hers allows her to pull off some very difficult colors."

"You know all of that is lost on me," he said. "However, I can see that she is beautiful."

Warmth flooded her. Such a stupid thing. To feel affected by this charade. But she wasn't entirely sure if she cared at all that it was a charade. What did it matter, really? Even playing a game like this was new. Feeling like she was the center—the focus—of male attention was something that she had scarcely gotten around to dreaming about.

She had been grappling with freedom. Both the cost of it and the gains. With who she wanted to be, apart from everything she'd been taught. Apart from the small rebellions she'd waged hidden in the mountains behind her house, listening to contraband music while reading forbidden books.

To find it especially appealing to link herself up to a

man, even in a temporary way. But now, beneath Renzo's black gaze, she found something deliciously enticing in it.

A swift, low kick of temptation hit her hard, making it difficult for her to breathe. And she couldn't even quite work out what the temptation was. It reminded her of walking past the bakery down in the town she'd grown up adjacent to, and seeing a row of sweets that looked delicious. Treats she knew she wouldn't be allowed to have.

That same feeling. Of wanting, feeling empty. Of that intense, unfair sense of deprivation that always followed.

Except, no one controlled her life now. If she wanted a cake, she could buy it and then she could eat it.

Which made her deeply conscious of the fact that if she wanted Renzo, she supposed she could have him, too.

But for the love of cake, she didn't know what she would do with him. Or what he would do with her if she reached out and tried to get a taste.

She took a deep breath, craning her neck, straightening her shoulders and doing her best to make herself look even more statuesque. She didn't know why. Maybe to inject herself with a little bit more pride, so she wasn't just standing there being subjected to the judgment of every person in the room.

It was so strange being the center of attention like this. She wasn't entirely certain she disliked it.

"That dress is spectacular. However, it is a bit too formal for dinner," Renzo said, sitting down in one of the armchairs that were placed up against the back wall. "What else is there?"

"Oh," Tierra said, turning around and facing the rack, pulling out a short, coral-colored dress that Esther had tried on earlier. "How about this?"

Renzo settled even deeper into the chair, his posture like that of a particularly jaded monarch. "Let's see it."

"Of course."

Esther found herself being turned so that she was facing away from Renzo, and then she felt the zipper on the gown give. She gasped, then froze, not quite sure what she was supposed to do next. If she should protest the fact that she was being undressed in front of a man who was a stranger to her, or if that would ruin the charade.

And then it didn't matter, because the green dress was pulling down at her feet, and her bare back and barely covered bottom were now fully exposed to Renzo.

"Very nice," he said, his voice rough. "Part of the new wardrobe?"

She knew he meant the black pair of lace panties she was wearing, and she wanted to turn around and tell him off for making this even more uncomfortable. Except, then she would have to turn around. And expose herself even further, and she wasn't going to do that. Instead, she decided that she would do her best to show him that she wasn't so easily toyed with.

"Yes," she said simply.

A few moments later the next dress was on and firmly in place. Then, she turned back to face Renzo, and her heart crawled up into her throat. Because as intense as he always looked, as much impact as those dark eyes always had on her, it was magnified now.

"Come closer," he said, his tone hard-edged, the command clearly nonnegotiable.

She swallowed hard, taking one unsteady step toward where Renzo was sitting. His dark gaze flicked away from Esther, landing on the style team. "Leave us," he said.

They did so, quickly and without a word. And when they were gone, it felt as though they had taken all the air out of the room with them.

"Do people always do what you ask?"

"Always," he said. "Closer."

She took another step toward him, trying to disguise the fact that her legs were shaking and that she had no idea how she was supposed to walk in heels that were tantamount to stilts.

He rested his elbow on the arm of the chair, propping his chin on his knuckles. "Of course, some people obey more quickly than others."

"Did you want me to break an ankle? Because I guarantee you if I walk any faster I'm going to."

He moved swiftly, his movements liquid, his grace making a mockery of her own uncertain clumsiness. He stood, reaching across the space between them and sweeping her up into his arms. Then he turned, depositing her in the chair he had occupied only a moment ago.

She pressed her hand to her heart, feeling the rapid flutter beneath her palm. Her throat was dry, her head feeling dizzy. Her body felt warm. As though she had been burned all over. His arms had been wrapped around her, her shoulder blades pressed up against that hard, broad expanse of his chest.

That was what stunned her most of all. Just how hard he was. There was no give in him at all. His body was as unbending as the rest of him.

He turned away from her, facing the rack of clothing and the stack of shoes that was beneath it. "If you cannot walk then you will not present a very convincing picture. We don't want you to look as though you were only polished today."

"Why? Why does it matter?"

"Because I associate with a very particular kind of woman. I do not need my parents thinking that I swooped in and corrupted some innocent, naive backpacker."

It took her a moment to process that. She wondered if

he really believed that she was naive and innocent. She was. It was just that he had never seemed particularly sold on that version of her.

"They would believe that?"

He laughed, not turning to look at her. "Oh, yes. Easily." Then he bent, picking up a pair of bejeweled, flat shoes before facing her again. He moved back to where she was sitting, dropping to his knees before her and making a seeming mockery of her earlier thought that he was unbending.

"What are you—"

He said nothing. Instead, he reached out, curling his fingers around the back of her knee. The warmth shocked her. Flooded her. He let his fingertips drift all the way down the length of her calf, the touch slow, much too slow. Something about it, about that methodical movement, seemed to catch her at the site of their contact and spark through the rest of her. Reckless. Uncontrollable.

She fought the urge to squirm in her seat. To do something to diffuse the strange energy that she was infused with. But she didn't want to betray herself. To betray that his touch made her feel anything.

He grabbed hold of the heel on her shoe and pulled it off slowly, those searching fingertips dragging along the bottom of her foot then as he removed the shoe.

She shivered. She couldn't help it.

He looked up then and a strange, knowing smile tilted the corner of his lips upward. It was the knowing that bothered her more than anything else. Because she was confused. Lost in a sea of swirling doubts and uncertainty, and he seemed to know exactly what she was feeling.

*You do, too. You aren't stupid.*

She gritted her teeth. Maybe. She really wished she were a little bit more stupid. She had tried to be. From the first moment she had laid eyes on him, and he had looked back at her, she had done her very best to be mystified by what all of the feelings inside her meant.

She wasn't going to give a name to them now. Not right now. Not when he was still touching her. Slipping the ornate flat shoe onto her foot, then moving on to the next. He repeated those same motions there. His fingertips hot and certain on her skin as he traced a line down to her ankle, removing the next stiletto and setting it aside.

"A little bit like Cinderella," she said, forcing the words through her dry throat.

Not that she'd been allowed to read fairy tales growing up, but a volume of them had been one of her very first smuggled titles.

"Except," he said, putting the second shoe in place, then straightening, "I am not Prince Charming."

"I didn't think you were."

"Good," he returned. "As long as you don't begin believing that I might be something I'm not."

"Why would I? I'm actually not just a stupid backpacker. I already told you that my family situation was difficult." She took a deep breath, trying to open up her lungs, trying to ease the tension in her chest. She wasn't bringing up her family for him. She was bringing them up for her. To remind her exactly why being bound to someone—anyone—was exactly what she didn't want.

She wanted freedom. She needed it. And this was a detour. She wouldn't allow herself to become convinced it was anything else.

She would enjoy this. The beautiful clothes, the expertly styled hair. She would enjoy his home. And maybe she would even allow herself to enjoy the strange twisting sensation that appeared in her stomach whenever he walked into a room. Because it was new. Because it was different. Because it was something so far removed from where she had come from.

But that was all it was. It was all it would ever be.

"But now," he said, looking down at her feet, "you will be able to walk into my parents' home tonight without falling on your face. That, I think, will be a much nicer effect."

He stood completely and held his hand out. She hesitated, because she knew that touching him again would reignite that burning sensation in the pit of her stomach she had when he'd touched her leg. But resisting would only reveal herself more. And she didn't want to do that.

And—she had to admit—she had perversely enjoyed it. Even though she knew it could never come to anything. Even though she knew there was nothing she could do beyond enjoying it as it was, as the start of a flame and nothing more, she sort of wanted to.

And so, she reached out, her fingertips brushing his palm. Then, his hand enveloped hers completely, and she found herself being pulled to her feet with shocking ease. In fact, he pulled her to her feet with such ease that she lost her footing, tipping forward and moving her hands up to brace herself, her palms pressing flat against that rock-hard chest.

He was so... He was so hot. And she could feel his heartbeat thundering beneath her touch. She hadn't expected that. She wondered if it was normal for him. For his heart to beat so fast. For it to feel so pronounced.

And then she had to wonder if it was related to her. Because her own heartbeat was thundering out of control, like a boulder rolling down a hill. It wasn't normal for her. It was because of him. And she couldn't pretend otherwise, not even to herself.

Was that why? Was that why his heart was beating so

fast? Because she was touching him? And if so, what did that mean?

It was that last question that had her pulling away from him as quickly as possible. She smoothed the front of her dress, doing her best to take care of any imaginary wrinkles that might be there, pouring her focus into that, because the alternative was looking at him.

"Yes," he said, his voice hard, rough, infused with much less ease than seemed typical for him. "Tonight will go very well, I think." And then he reached out, taking hold of her chin with his thumb and forefinger. He forced her to look at him, stealing that small respite she had attempted to take for herself. His eyes burned, and she wasn't sure if she could still somehow sense his heartbeat, or if it was just her own, pounding heavily in her ears. "But you will have to find a way to keep yourself from flinching every time I touch you."

Then, he dropped his hand, turning away from her and walking out of the room, leaving her alone. Leaving her to wonder if she had imagined that response in him because of the strength of her own reaction, or if—somehow—she had created movement in the mountain.

## CHAPTER SIX

DINNER AT HIS parents was always infused with a bit of dramatic flair. Tonight was no exception. They were greeted by his parents' housekeeper, their coats taken by another member of staff and then led into the sitting room by yet another.

Of course, his mother would not make an appearance until it was time to sit down at the table. He had a feeling it was calculated this time, even more than usual. That she was preparing herself for the unveiling of Renzo's new fiancée.

His father would go along with his mother's plan. Mostly because he had no desire to have something thrown at his head. Not that his mother had behaved with such hysterics for a great many years. But everyone knew she possessed the capacity for such things, and so they tended to behave with a bit of deference for it.

He turned to look at Esther, who was regarding the massive, Baroque setting with unconcealed awe. "You will have to look a bit more inured to your surroundings. As far as my parents know you have been with me for at least a couple of months, which means you will have been at events like this with me before."

"This place is like a museum," she said, keeping her tone hushed, her dark eyes glittering with wonder. It did something to him. Something to his chest. Unlike earlier, when she had done something to him in parts much lower.

"Yes," he said, "it is, really. A museum of my family's achievements. Of all of the things they have managed to collect over the centuries. I told you, my parents were very proud of our name and our heritage. Of what it means to be Valentis." He gritted his teeth. "Blood is everything to them."

It was why they would accept Esther. Why they would accept the situation. Because except in extreme circumstances, they valued their bloodline in their heritage.

He deliberately kept himself from thinking of the one time they had not.

"Renzo." He turned at the sound of his sister's voice, surprised to see her standing there with her husband, Cristian, at her side, Renzo's niece held securely in her father's arms.

"Allegra," he said, standing and walking across the room to drop a kiss on his younger sister's cheek. He extended his hand for Cristian, shaking it firmly before touching his niece's cheek. "I did not know you would be here."

"Neither did we."

"Did you fly from Spain for dinner?"

Cristian lifted a shoulder. "When your mother demands an audience, it is best not to refuse, as I'm sure you know."

"Indeed."

He turned and looked at Esther, who was still sitting on the settee, her hands folded in her lap, her shoulders curved inward, as though she were trying to disappear. "Allegra, Cristian, this is my fiancée, Esther Abbott."

His words seemed to jolt Esther out of her internal reclusion.

"Hello," she said, getting to her feet, stumbling slightly as she did. "You must be… Well, I'm not really sure."

Allegra shot him a questioning glance. "Allegra Acosta. Formerly Valenti. I'm Renzo's younger sister. This is my husband, Cristian."

"Nice to meet you," she said, keeping her hands folded firmly in front of her but nodding her head. He was hardly going to correct her, or direct her to do something different from what she had done, but he could see that coaching would be required in the future.

"It seems the family will all be here," he said. "Such a surprise."

"Engaged. You're engaged. That's why Mother called us and told us to get on Cristian's private jet, I imagine."

"Most definitely," Renzo returned.

"You didn't tell me," Allegra said.

"In fairness to me, you did not tell me that you were expecting my best friend's baby until it became unavoidable. You can hardly lecture me on not serving up a particular piece of news immediately."

His sister's face turned scarlet, and he looked back at Esther, who was watching the exchange with rapt attention. "Don't pay attention to him," Allegra said to Esther. "He very much likes to be shocking. And he likes to make me mad."

"That seems in keeping with what I know about him," Esther said.

Cristian laughed at that. "You two can't have been together very long," he said. "But it does seem you have a handle on him."

Esther looked down. "I wouldn't say that."

Renzo poured himself a drink, feeling slightly sorry for Esther that he could not offer her the same. Especially given what he was about to do. "Since Mother didn't tell you the great news of my engagement, I imagine she didn't tell you I have other news."

"No," Allegra and Cristian said together.

"Esther and I are expecting a baby." He reached out, putting his arm around Esther's shoulders, rubbing his thumb up and down her arm when he felt her go stiff. That didn't help, but he knew that it needled her. So, he would have to take that as consolation.

Allegra said nothing, Cristian's expression one of almost comedic stillness. Finally, it was Cristian who spoke. "Congratulations. Start catching up on your sleep now."

Allegra still said nothing.

"I can see you're completely stunned by the good news," he said.

"Well, yes. I know you've made many declarations to me about how you intend to be shocking at all times, so I don't know why I'm surprised. Actually, I heavily resent my surprise. I should be immune to any sort of shock where you're concerned."

Of course, she wasn't. Being his younger sister, Allegra always seemed to want to believe the best of him. Which was a very nice thing, in its way. But he was a constant disappointment to her. He knew that his marriage to Ashley had been something more than a shock. Although, why, he didn't know. He had told her, in no uncertain terms, that he intended to marry the most unsuitable, shocking woman that he could find.

That was one that had backfired on him.

"Truly, little sister, you should know me better than that by now. Anyway, let us refrain from speaking of the other ways in which I've shocked you in front of Esther. She's still under the illusion that I'm something of a gentleman."

Esther looked at him, her expression bland. "I can assure you I'm not."

Cristian and Allegra seemed to find that riotously amusing. Mostly, he imagined, because they thought she was being dry. In fact, he had a feeling Esther was being perfectly sincere. She was sincere. That was something he was grappling with. Because he didn't know very many sincere people.

He was much more accustomed to those who were cynical. Who approached the world with a healthy bit of opportunism. It was the sincere people who dumbfounded him. Mostly, because he couldn't figure out a way to relate to them. He couldn't anticipate them.

Seeing her earlier today trying on all of those clothes, the way she had looked at him when he had touched her leg, when he had bent down to change her shoes, had been something of a revelation. Until then he had still been skeptical of her. Of her story, of who she claimed to be.

But who she seemed to present was exactly who she was. A somewhat naive creature who was from a world entirely apart from the one she was in now. Her reaction to his parents' house only reinforced that. He had watched her closely upon entry. If she were a gold digger, he felt he would have seen a moment—even if it was only a moment—where she had looked triumphant. Where she had fully understood the prize that she was inheriting.

Frankly, the position he had put her in gave her quite a bit of leverage for taking advantage. Yes, DNA tests would prove that the child wasn't hers, but who knew how a ruling might go in Italy where there were no laws to support surrogacy. She was the woman who carried the child, and she would give birth to the child. He imagined that legally there was no way she would walk away with nothing.

And he had offered to marry her. Another way in which she could take advantage of him and his money. And yet she had not seemed excited by that either.

That didn't mean things wouldn't change, but for now,

he was forced to reconcile with the fact that she might be the rarest of all creatures. Someone who was what she said.

"Excellent," Allegra said to Esther. "I would hate for you to marry my brother while thinking he was well behaved."

Spurred on by his earlier ruminations, he turned his head, nuzzling the tender skin on Esther's neck, just beneath her jawline. "Of course," he said, allowing his lips to brush against her, "Esther is well aware of how wicked I can be."

He looked up, trying to gauge her response. Her burnished skin was dark pink beneath, a wild, fevered look in her eye. "Yes," she said, her voice higher than usual. "We do know each other. Quite well. We are… We're having a baby. So…"

"Right," Allegra said.

Just then, a servant came in, interrupting the awkward exchange. "Excuse me," the man said. "Your mother has asked me to 'come and fetch you for dinner.'"

Likely, those were his mother's exact words.

Keeping his hand on Esther's lower back, he led the charge out of the room and toward the dining hall. He could feel her growing stiffer and stiffer beneath his touch the closer they got, almost as if she could sense his mother. He wouldn't be surprised. His mother radiated ice, and openly telegraphed her difficulty to be pleased.

"Take a breath," he whispered in her ear just before they walked in. She complied, her shoulders lifting with a great gasp. "See that you don't die before dessert."

And then he propelled her inside.

His mother was there, dressed in sequins, looking far too young to have two grown children, one grandchild and another on the way. His father was there, looking every bit his age, stern-faced and distinguished, and likely a portrait of Renzo's own fate in thirty years.

"Hello," his mother said, not standing, which Renzo knew was calculated in some way or another. "So nice to meet you, Esther," his mother said, using Esther's first name, which he had no doubt was as calculated as the rest. "Allegra, Cristian, so glad you could come. And that you brought my favorite grandchild."

"Your only grandchild," Allegra said, taking her seat while Cristian set about to setting their daughter in a booster seat that had already been put in place for her.

All of this was like salt in a wound. He loved his niece, but there was a particular kind of pain that always came when he was around small children. And when his parents said things like this…about their only grandchild… that pain seemed insurmountable.

"Not for long, though," Allegra continued. "Unless Renzo hasn't told you?"

"He has not. Good. Well, at least now we're all up to speed." His mother gave Renzo a very pointed look. "Do you have any other surprises for us?"

"Not at the moment," he said.

Dinner went on smoothly, their mother and father filling up most of the conversation, and Renzo allowing his brother-in-law to take any of the gaps that appeared. Cristian was a duke, and his title made him extremely interesting to Renzo and Allegra's parents.

Then suddenly, his father's focus turned to Renzo. "I suppose we will see both you and Esther at the charity art exhibit in New York in two weeks?"

Damn. He had forgotten about that. His father was a big one for philanthropy, and he insisted that Renzo make appearances at these types of events. Not because his father believed firmly in charity in a philosophical sense, but because he believed in being seen as someone who did. Oh, he wasn't completely cold-blooded, and truly, it didn't matter either way. A good amount of money made it into needy hands regardless.

But bringing Esther to New York, having her prepared to attend such a land mine–laden event with very little preparation was… Well, just thinking about it was difficult.

More than just the Esther complication, there was always the Jillian complication. Or worse, Samantha. They split their time between Italy and the States, so the probability of seeing them was…high.

But he'd weathered that countless times. Esther was his chief concern. She would probably end up hiding under one of the buffet tables, or perhaps eating a bowl of chocolate mousse on the floor. Thankfully, it would be at night, so there would be no sunbeams for her to warm herself beneath.

"Of course," he said, answering as quickly as possible, before Esther opened her mouth. He had to make it seem as though they had discussed this. That he had not in fact forgotten about the existence of this event—one that he attended every year—due to the fact that he had been shocked by the news of a stranger carrying his child.

"Excellent," his father said. "I do find that it's much better for a man such as yourself to attend with a date."

"Why is that?"

"So you aren't on the prowl for women when you should be on the prowl for business connections."

That shot from his father surprised him. Especially in front of Esther. His father was typically the more restrained of his two parents. Still, he was hardly going to let the old man see that it had surprised him. "You live in the Dark Ages, Father," he said. "Sometimes, women are in high-powered positions of business, in which case, my being single helps quite a bit. However, Esther will not be an impediment, on that you are correct."

"Certainly not," his father said. "If anything, she will be something of an attraction to those jaded big fish you intend to catch."

"Are you going to be there, Father?"

"No. When I said I hoped to see you there, I meant only that I hope to see your photograph in the newspaper."

Renzo couldn't help but laugh at that. And after that, conversation went smoothly through dessert. At least, until they were getting ready to go. A staff member waylaid Esther, a maneuver that Renzo fully took notice of only when his father cornered him near the front door.

"I do hope this isn't some sort of elaborate joke like your last relationship seems to have been," his father said.

"Why would it be?"

"She is a lovely girl. She's a far cry from the usual vacuous model types you choose to associate yourself with. I had to cut ties with one of my grandchildren already, Renzo, lest you forget."

"You didn't have to. You felt it was necessary at the time and you convinced me the same was true. Don't pretend that you have regrets now, old man," Renzo said, his tone hard. "Not when you were so emphatic about the need for it all those years ago."

"What I'm saying is that you best marry this girl. And that marriage best stick. A divorce, Renzo. You had a divorce. And a child outside of wedlock that none of us can ever acknowledge."

"What will you do if I disappoint you again, Father? Find the secret to immortality and deny me my inheritance?"

"Your brother-in-law is more than able to take over the

remainder of the business that is not yet under your control. If you don't want to lose dominion over the Valenti Empire upon the event of my death, I suggest you don't disappoint me."

His father moved away from him swiftly then, and Esther came to join him standing by the door. She looked like a deer caught in the headlights, blindsided completely by the entire evening.

And he knew he now had no choice in the matter. This farce would not be enough. It had to be more. His father was threatening his future, and not just his, that of his child.

Esther Abbott was going to have to become his wife, whether she wanted to or not.

And he knew exactly how to accomplish it. He had seen the way she had reacted to his touch back at his villa. He knew that she wasn't immune to him. And a woman like her, naive, vulnerable, would not be immune to the emotions that would come with the physical seduction.

It was ruthless, even for him. He preferred honesty. Preferred to let the women he got involved with know exactly what they were in for. Preferred to let them know that emotion was never going to be on the table. That love was never going to be a factor.

But he would offer her marriage, and she could hardly ask for more than that. In this instance, what would the harm be?

There was no other option. He was going to have to make Esther Abbott fall in love with him. And the only way to accomplish that would be seduction.

"Come on, Esther," he said, holding out his arm, "it is time for us to go home."

# CHAPTER SEVEN

ESTHER WAS USED to the breakneck pace of working in the bar. Going out every night and working until closing time was demanding. But the routine of getting ready, polishing herself from head to toe, so that she could go out with Renzo for a dinner in Rome, was something else entirely. And it was almost no less exhausting.

Being on show was such a strange thing. She was used to being ignored. Invisible.

But two nights ago they had gone to his parents' house, and the scrutiny she had been put under there had been unlike anything she'd experienced since she'd lived at home and it had always seemed as though her father was trying to look beneath her skin for evidence of defiance, sin or vice.

Then, last night they had gone out again to a very nice restaurant, and Renzo had explained to her exactly what the charity event in New York was, and how she would be accompanying him.

Tonight, they were going to another dinner, though Renzo had not explained the purpose of this one. And it made her slightly nervous. He had also made her a doctor's appointment at a private clinic, not the one that Ashley had used. But one that he had chosen himself. Based on, he claimed, the doctor's reputation for discretion.

It seemed ridiculous to have to get dressed up for a doctor's appointment, but Renzo had explained that they would be going out afterward, so she would have to dress appropriately for dinner beforehand.

So, here she was now, sitting in the back of a limousine, being driven out to her appointment where Renzo was supposed to meet her. She was wearing lipstick.

The limo came to a stop, and she was deposited in front of a building that seemed far too polished to be a simple medical clinic. But then, Ashley had been aiming for a different kind of discretion when they had gone to the surrogacy clinic.

The driver opened the door for her, and she realized that she had to get out. Even though she just wanted to keep sitting there. For one horrifying second she wondered if she was going to go into the clinic, lie down on the doctor's table, and he was going to tell her the baby was gone.

For some reason, in that moment, the thought made her feel bereft. She wasn't sure why it should. Maybe for Renzo? Because he was rearranging his life for this child?

*Or maybe, it's because you aren't ready to let go of the baby?*

No, that was unthinkable. She wasn't attached to this. She just felt natural protectiveness. It was a hormone thing. She was sure of that. But she couldn't remember feeling sick for the last couple of days, not even a little bit of nausea, and she wondered if that was indicative of something bad. She wondered that even while she spoke to the woman at the front desk and was ushered into a private waiting room.

She wrung her hands, jiggling her leg, barely able to enjoy the opulence of the surroundings. She tried. She really did. Because she had purposed to be on this journey.

To enjoy this little window into something that would always and forever be outside her daily experiences.

She didn't know when she had started to care. At least not in a way that extended beyond the philosophical. That extended past her feeling like she had to preserve the life inside her out of a sense of duty. She only knew that it had.

Thankfully, she didn't have a whole lot of time to ruminate on that, because just then, Renzo entered the room. There was something wild and stormy in his gaze that she couldn't guess at. But then, that was nothing new. She didn't feel like she could ever guess what he was thinking.

"Where is the doctor?" He didn't waste any time assessing the situation and deciding it was lacking.

"I don't know. But I imagine it won't be much longer."

"It is a crime that you have been kept waiting at all," he said, his tone terse.

She hugged herself just a little bit more tightly, anxiety winding itself around her stomach. "You weren't here anyway. It didn't matter particularly whether or not the doctor materialized before you, did it?"

"You could have been preparing for the exam."

Esther didn't say anything. She could only wonder if Renzo was experiencing similar feelings to hers. It seemed strange to think that he would, but then, also not so strange. It was his baby. It actually made more sense than her being nervous.

"Ms. Abbott," a woman said, sticking her head through the door. "The doctor is ready to see you now."

Esther took a deep breath, pushing herself into a standing position. She was aware of walking toward the door on unsteady legs, and then hyperaware of Renzo reaching out and cupping her elbow, steadying her. "I'm fine," she said.

"You look like a very light breeze could knock you over."

"I'm *fine*," she reiterated. Even though she wasn't certain if she was.

Renzo let the line of conversation go, but he did not let go of her arm. Instead, he held on to her all the way down the private hallway and into the exam room.

"Remove your clothing and put on this gown," the nurse said. "The doctor will be in in just a few moments."

Esther looked at Renzo, her gaze pointed. But he didn't seem to take the hint.

"Can you leave?" she asked, the moment the nurse was out of sight.

"Why should I leave? You are my fiancée, after all."

"Your fiancée in name only. You and I both know that this child was not conceived in the…in the…the usual way that children are conceived. You don't have any right to look at me while I'm undressing. I couldn't say that in front of the stylist the other day, but I will say it now."

"I will turn," he said, his tone dry. And he did.

She took a deep breath, her eyes glued to his broad back, and she began to remove her clothing. It didn't matter that he couldn't *see* her. The feeling of undressing in the same room as a man was so shockingly intimate.

Everything had happened so quickly during her little makeover the other day. And while she had been embarrassed that he was looking at her body, she hadn't fully processed all of her feelings. Right now, she could process them all a bit too well.

From the dull thud of her heart, to the fluttering of her pulse at the base of her throat. The way that her fingers felt clumsy, numb, but everything else on her body felt hypersensitive and so very warm, tingly.

She could sense him. More than just seeing him standing in front of her, he felt all around her. As though he took up every corner of the room, even though she knew such a thing wasn't possible.

Finally, she got all of her clothes off, and stood there for a moment. Just a moment. Long enough to process the fact that she was standing naked in a room with this powerful man, who was dressed in a perfectly tailored suit.

It was such a strange contrast. She had never felt more vulnerable, more exposed or…stronger, than she did in that moment. And she could not understand all of those contrasting things coming together to create *one* feeling.

She picked up the hospital gown and slipped it onto her shoulders, then got up onto the plush table that was so very different from the other table she had been on just a few months ago. "This is different," she said. "From the clinic in Santa Firenze."

He turned then, not asking if he could. But she had a feeling that Renzo was not a man accustomed to asking for much. "In what way?"

"Well, I get the feeling that Ashley was doing her best to keep all of this from getting back to you. So, she opted for discreet. But not like this. It was…rustic?"

His lip curled. "Excellent. She took you to a bargain fertility clinic." His hands curled into fists. "If I ever get my hands on her…"

"Don't. The fact that she is who she is is punishment enough, isn't it?"

He laughed. "I suppose it is."

There was a firm knock on the door, followed by the door opening quickly. Then, the doctor—a small woman with her hair pulled back into a tight bun—walked into the room. "Ms. Abbott, Mr. Valenti, it's very nice to meet you. I'm very pleased to be helping you along with your pregnancy."

After introductions were made, and Esther's vitals were

taken, the woman had Esther lie down on the table, then she placed a towel over Esther's lap and pushed the hospital gown up to the bottom of her rib cage.

"We're going to do an ultrasound. To establish viability, listen to the heartbeat and get a look at the baby."

Anxiety gripped her. This was the moment of truth, she supposed. The moment where she found out if those prickling fears she'd had in the waiting room were in any way factual. Or if they were just vague waves of anxiety, connected to nothing more but her general distrust of the situation.

She really hoped it was the second.

The doctor squirted some warm gel onto her stomach, then placed the Doppler on her skin. She moved the wand around until Esther caught sight of a vague fluttering on the monitor next to her. Her breath left her body in a great gust, relief washing over her. "That's the heart," she asked, "isn't it?"

"Yes," the doctor said, flipping a switch and letting a steady thumping sound fill the room. "There it is."

It was strange, like a rhythmic swishing, combined with a watery sound in the back. The Doppler moved, and the sound faded slightly.

"I'm just trying to get a good look." She kept on moving the Doppler around, and new images flashed onto the screen, new angles of the baby that she carried. But Esther couldn't make heads or tails of any of it. She had no experience with ultrasounds.

"Do either of you have a history of twins in your family?"

The question hit Esther square in the chest, and she struggled to come up with any response that wasn't simply *why*.

She didn't. But she knew that the question didn't actually pertain to her, since the child she was carrying wasn't hers. "I…"

"No," Renzo said, his tone definitive. "However… The baby was conceived elsewhere through artificial means. If that has any impact on what you're about to say."

"Well, that does increase the odds of such things," the doctor said. "And that is in fact what it looks like here. Twins."

All of the relief that had just washed through Esther was gone now, replaced by wave after wave of thundering terror. Twins? There was no way she could be carrying twins. That was absurd.

Here she had been worried that she had lost one baby, that they would look inside her womb and see nothing, when they had actually found an extra baby.

"I don't understand," Esther said. "I don't understand at all. I don't understand how it could be twins. I've been to the doctor before to have the pregnancy checked on…"

"These things are easy to miss early on. Especially if they were just looking at heartbeats with the Doppler."

She felt heat rush through her face. "Yes," she confirmed.

"I understand that it's a bit of a shock."

"It's fine," Renzo said, his tone hard, belying that calm statement. "I have more than enough means to handle such things. I'm not at all concerned. Of course we are able to care for twins."

"Everything looks good," the doctor said, pulling the Doppler off Esther's stomach and wiping her skin free of gel. "Of course, we will want to monitor you closely as twins are considered a more high-risk pregnancy. You're young. And all of your vitals look good. I don't see why you shouldn't have a very successful pregnancy."

Esther was vaguely aware of nodding, while Renzo

simply stood there. Like a statue straight from a Roman temple.

Seeing that neither of them had anything to say, the doctor nodded. "I'll leave you two to discuss."

As soon as the doctor left, Esther sagged back onto the table, flattening herself entirely, going utterly limp. "I can't believe it."

"You can't believe it? You're the one who intends to leave. Why would it concern you?"

"*I'm* the one who has to carry a litter," she shot back.

"Twins are hardly a litter."

"Well, that's easy for you to say. You're not the one gestating them."

He looked stunned. Pale beneath his burnished skin. "Indeed not." He turned away from her. "Get dressed. We have reservations."

"I know I do. I have several reservations!"

"For dinner."

"You're not seriously suggesting that we just go out to dinner as though nothing's happened?"

"I am suggesting exactly that," he said through gritted teeth. "Get dressed. We are leaving to go to dinner."

She growled and got off the table, moving back over to her clothes on unsteady legs. She picked up the lacy underwear that had been provided by Renzo's stylist and slipped them up her legs, not even bothering to enjoy the lush feel of the fabric as she had been doing every other time before.

There was no pausing for lushness when you'd just found out you were carrying not one, but *two* babies.

She made quick work of the rest of her clothes. At least, as quick work as she could possibly make of them with her trembling fingers. "I'm ready," she snapped.

"Very good. Now, let us cease with the dramatics and go to dinner."

He all but hauled her out of the office, taking her to his sports car, where he yanked open the passenger-side door and held it for her.

She looked up at him, at his inscrutable face that was very much like a cloudy sky. She could tell a storm was gathering there, but she couldn't quite make out why. Then, she jerked her focus away from him and got into the car, clasping her hands tightly in her lap and staring straight ahead.

He closed the door, then got in on his side, bringing the engine to life with an angry roar and tearing out of the parking lot like the hounds of hell were on his heels.

"You dare call me dramatic?" she asked. "If this isn't dramatic, I don't know what is."

"I only just found out that I'm having two children, not one. If any of us is entitled to a bit of drama…"

"You seem to discount my role in this," she fired back. "At every turn, in fact, you treat me as nothing more than a vessel. Not understanding at all that there is a bit of work that goes into this. Some labor, if you will."

"Modern medicine makes it all quite simple."

"That is…well and truly spoken only like a man. What about what this is going to do to my body? It's going to leave me with stretch marks and then some." She didn't actually care about that, but she felt like poking him. Goading him. She wanted to make him feel something. Because for whatever reason this revelation had rocked her entire world, made her feel as though she herself had been tilted on her very axis. She didn't think he had a right to be more upset than she was. And maybe that wasn't fair. Maybe it was hormones. But she didn't particularly care.

"I will get you whatever surgery you want in order to return your body to its former glory. If you're concerned about what lovers will be able to get afterward, don't be."

That statement was almost laughable.

"I am not concerned about lovers," she said. "My life is not dependent on what other people think. Been there, done that, got rid of the overly starched ankle-length dresses. But what about what *I* think?"

"You are *impossible*. And a contradiction."

He drove on with a bit too much fervor through the narrow streets, practically careening around every corner, forcing her to grip the door handle as they made their way through town.

They stopped in front of a small café, and he got out, handing the keys to a valet in front of the door. It took her a moment to realize that he was not coming around to open the door for her. She huffed, doing it herself and getting out, gathering the fabric of her skirt and getting herself in order once she was fully straightened.

"That was not very gentlemanly," she said, rounding the front of the car and taking as big a step as her skirt would allow.

"I am very sorry. It has been said that I am perhaps not very gentlemanly. In fact, I believe it was said recently by you."

"Perhaps you should listen to the feedback."

He wrapped his arm around her waist, the heat from his hand shocking. His fingertips rested just beneath the curve of her breast, making her heart beat faster, stronger.

"I'm *very* sorry," he said, his voice husky. "Please say you'll forgive me. At least in time for the paparazzi to catch up with us. I would not want pictures of our dinner to go into the paper with you looking stormy."

"Oh, perish the thought. We cannot have anything damaging your precious reputation."

"Our association is entirely for my reputation. You will not ruin this. If you do, I promise I will make you pay. I will take money out of our agreement so quickly it will make your head spin. You do not want to play games with me, Esther."

He whispered those words in her ear, and for all the world he would look like a lover telling secrets. They would never guess that it was a man on the brink issuing threats.

It galled her that they worked.

He walked them inside, without being stopped by anyone, and went to a table that he had undoubtedly sat at many times before. He did pull her chair out for her, making a gentlemanly show there as he had failed to do at the car.

"Sparkling water," he said to the waiter when he came by.

"What if I wanted something else?" she asked, just to continue prodding at him.

"Your options are limited, as you cannot drink alcohol."

"Still. Maybe I wanted juice."

"Did you want juice?" he asked, his tone inflexible.

"No," she said, feeling defeated by that.

"Then behave yourself."

He took control like that with the rest of the dinner, proceeding to order her food—because he knew what the best dishes were at the restaurant—and not listening to any of her protestations.

She didn't know why she should find that particularly surprising. He had done that from the beginning. She had tried to come to him, had tried to do things on her own terms, but he had taken the reins at almost every turn.

Suddenly, sitting there in this restaurant that was so far outside her experience—would have been outside her scope for imagination only a few weeks earlier—she had the sensation that she was being pulled down beneath the surface. That she was out in the middle of the sea, unable to grab hold of anything that might anchor her.

She was afraid she might drown.

She took a deep breath, tried to disguise the fact that it was just short of a gasp.

Finally, their dessert plates were cleared, and Esther felt like she might be able to approach breathing normally again. Soon, they would be back at the villa. And while she still found his palatial home overwhelming, it was at least a familiar sort of overwhelming. Or rather, it had become so over the past few days.

Then, she looked up at him, and that brief moment of sanity melted into nothing. There was a strange look in his eye, one of purpose and determination. And if there was one thing she knew about Renzo it was that he was immovable at the best of times. Infused with an extra sense of purpose and he would be all-consuming.

She didn't want to be consumed by him. Not in any capacity. Looking into his dark eyes now, an answering twist low in her stomach, she wasn't certain she could avoid it.

He reached into the interior pocket of his jacket then, his dark eyes never wavering from hers, and then he got out of his chair, kneeling in front of her. She couldn't breathe. If she had had the sensation of drowning before, it had become something even more profound now. Like being swept up in a tide that she couldn't swim against. The effect those eyes always had on her.

The effect he seemed to have on her.

She was supposed to be stronger than this. Smarter than this. Immune to the charms of men. Especially men like him. Men who sought to control the world around them, from the people who populated their surroundings, to the homes they lived in, all the way down to the elements. She imagined that if a weather report disagreed with Renzo, he would rail at that until it changed its mind.

She knew all about men like that. Knew all about the importance of staying away from them.

Her mother had been normal once. That was something Esther wasn't supposed to know. But she had found the pictures. Had seen photographs of her mother as a young girl, dressed in the trends of the day, looking very much like any average girl might have.

She had never been able to reconcile those photographs of the past with the woman she had grown up with. Quiet. Dowdy. So firmly under the command of her husband that she never dared to oppose him in any way at all.

It had been a mystery both to her father and her mother that Esther had possessed any bit of rebelliousness at all. But she had. She did. And if there was one thing Esther feared at all in the world, it was losing that. Becoming that drawn, colorless woman who had raised her.

Love had done it to her. Or more truthfully, control carefully disguised as love.

It was so easy to confuse the two, she knew. She knew because she'd done it. Because she'd imagined her father had been overbearing out of a sense of protectiveness.

Those thoughts flashed through her mind like a strobe light. Fast, confusing, blinding, obscuring what was happening in front of her.

She blinked, trying to get a grip on herself. Trying to get a grip on the moment. It wouldn't benefit her at all to lose it now.

"Esther," he said, his voice transforming itself into something velvet, softening the command that had been in it only moments before. Brushing itself against her skin, a lush seduction rather than a hard demand.

He was dangerous. Looking at him now, she was reminded of that. She told herself over and over again as he opened the box he had taken out of his coat pocket and held it out to her. As he revealed the diamond ring inside.

He was dangerous. This wasn't real. This was something else. A window into a life she would never have. This was experience. Experience without consequence. She was pregnant. She was having twins. And she was playing at being rich and fancy with the father of those twins. But they weren't her babies. Not really. And he wasn't her fiancé. Wasn't her man at all.

That was a good thing. A very good thing. She didn't want anything else. Not from him. Not from anyone. She couldn't sustain this.

But she had to go along with this. And she had to remember exactly what it was, all the while smiling and doing nothing to disrupt the facade. Which, he had reminded her, was the most important thing. She could understand it. On a surface level, she could understand. But right now, she felt jumbled up. And she hated it.

Still, when he took the ring out of the box and then took her hand in his, sliding the piece of jewelry onto her fourth finger, she felt breathless. Felt like it was something more than a show, which proved all the weakness inside her. All the weakness she had long been afraid was there.

"Will you marry me?" he finished finally, those last words the darkest, the softest of all.

This was a moment she had never even fantasized about. Ever. She had never seen marriage or relationships as anything to aspire to. But this felt... This felt like nothing she had ever known before. And the question Renzo was asking seemed to be completely different from the one her father had undoubtedly asked her mother more than twenty years ago.

Of course it was. Because it was a ruse. But more than

that, this whole world might as well exist on another planet entirely.

*But that doesn't make him less dangerous. It doesn't make him a different creature. He's still controlling. Still hard.*

*And he doesn't love you.*

Her heart slammed hard against her rib cage. "Yes," she said, both to him and to the voice inside her.

She knew Renzo didn't love her. She didn't want Renzo to love her. Not like that. Love like that wasn't freedom. It was oppression.

She was confused. All messed up because of the doctor's appointment today. Because of the revelations that had resulted. Because of her hormones and because she was—frankly—in over her head.

That was the truth of it. She, Esther Abbott, long-cloistered weirdo who knew very little about the outside world and a very definite virgin, had no business being here with a man like Renzo. She had absolutely no business being pregnant at all, and she really shouldn't be on the receiving end of a proposal.

It was no great mystery that she felt like a jumble of feelings and pain while her head logically knew exactly what was happening. Her brain wasn't confused at all. Not at all.

But there was something weighty about the diamond on her finger. Something substantial about her yes that she couldn't quite quantify, and didn't especially want to.

It was the confusion inside her, tumbling around like clothes in that rickety old dryer at the hostel, that kept her from preparing herself for what happened next. At least, that was what she told herself later.

Because before she could react, before she could catch her breath, move or prepare herself in any way, Renzo brought his hand up and cupped her cheek, sliding his thumb over her cheekbone. It was like putting a lit match up against a pool of gasoline. It set off a trail of fire from that point of contact down to the center of her body.

And while she was grappling with that, added to everything else, he closed the distance between them and his mouth met hers.

Everything burned to ash then, bright white and cleansing. Every concern, every thought, everything gone from her mind in a flash as his lips moved over hers. That was what surprised her the most. The movement.

She hadn't imagined there was quite so much activity to being kissed. But there was. The shift of his hand against her face, sliding back to her hair, his lips learning the shape of hers and giving to accommodate that.

Then, his lips, lips she had never imagined could soften, did. And after that they parted, the shocking, wet slide of his tongue at the seam of her mouth undoing her completely. It set off an earthquake in her midsection that battled through her, leaving her devastated, hollowed out, an aching sense of being unfulfilled making her feel scraped raw.

She didn't know what to do. And so, she did the one thing she had always feared she might do when facing down a man like this. She gave. She allowed him to part her lips, allowed him to take it deeper.

Another tremor shook her, skating down her spine and rattling her frame. She didn't even fight it. She didn't even hate it.

When she had left home, when she had decided that she was going to go out into the world and see everything that was there for her to take. When she had decided finally to sort through what her parents had taught her and what was true, when she had decided to find out who she was, not who she had been commanded to be, this had never factored in.

She had never imagined herself in a situation like this. In the back of her mind she had imagined that someday she would want to explore physical desire. But it had been shoved way, way to the back of her mind. It had been a priority. Because so much of her life had been about being bound to a group of people. Being underneath the authority of someone else.

So, she had wanted to remain solitary. And at some point, she had imagined she might make a group of friends. When she decided to settle. At some point, she had imagined she might want to find a man for a romance. But it had been so far out ahead of what she had wanted in the immediate.

Freedom. A taste of the world that had always been hidden from her. Strange food and strange air. Strange sun on skin that had always been covered before.

Suddenly, all of that was obscured. Suddenly, all of it paled in comparison to this. Which was hotter than any sun, more powerful than any air she'd ever tasted—from the salted tang of the Mediterranean to the damp grit of London—and brighter than any flavor she'd ever had on her tongue.

It was Renzo. Pure, undiluted. Everything that gaze had promised her from the moment she had first seen him. The way he had immobilized her with just a glance had been only a hint. Like when a sliver of sun was just barely visible behind a dark cloud.

The cloud had just moved. Revealing all of the brilliance behind it. Brilliance that, she had a feeling, would be permanently damaging if she allowed herself to linger in it for too long.

But just a little while longer. Just a moment. One more

breath. She could skip one more breath for another taste of Renzo's mouth.

He pulled back then, dropping one more kiss on her lips before separating from her completely. And then he curled his fingers around hers, pulling her from her chair and up against his chest. "I think," he said, a roughness in his voice that had been absent only a moment ago, "that it is time for us to go home, don't you?"

"Yes," she said. Because there was nothing else to say. Because anything more intelligent would require three times the brain cells than she currently possessed.

And then he took her hand and led her from the restaurant. The car was waiting against the curb when they got back, and she didn't even ask how he had made sure they wouldn't have to wait.

He hadn't made a phone call. She hadn't caught any sort of signal between himself and a member of the restaurant staff. It looked like magic. More of the magic that seemed to shimmer from Renzo, that seemed to have a way of obscuring things. At least, as she saw them.

She had to get herself together. She told herself that, all the way home from the restaurant, and as she stepped into the house. And then she told herself that again when she realized that she had just referred to Renzo's home as her own in her mind.

She wanted to look at the ring on her finger. To examine the way the landscape of her own body had changed since he had put it on. She had never owned a piece of jewelry like that. She had bought a few fake, funky pieces when she had left home. Because she liked the way they jingled, and she liked the little bit of flash. Something to remind her of her freedom.

But diamonds had been a bit outside her purview.

She stole a quick glance down, the gem glittering in the light.

Then, it was as though a bucket of water had been dumped over her head. Suddenly, the haze that she had been under diminished. And once it did, she was angry.

"What were you thinking? Why didn't you warn me?"

# CHAPTER EIGHT

RENZO DID NOT have the patience to deal with Esther and her pique right at the moment. His world felt like it had been completely turned on end. He was not having one child, but two. He could hardly sort through that.

He had opted to carry on with his plan, as though there had been no surprises at the doctor's today. He had continued on with his plan to propose to her at one of the more high-profile restaurants in Rome, where they would be sure to have their picture taken, so they could be splashed out on the tabloids. The same tabloids that had covered his incredibly public divorce from Ashley just recently.

It had been calculated. Very specifically. To set the stage so the people would believe this relationship was real. So that they would believe this pregnancy had come about in a natural way.

What he had not counted on was the kiss. Or more specifically, how it had affected him. Yes, he had known that Esther was beautiful. He had also known that he was not immune to that beauty. When he had watched Tierra dress her just the other day, he had been captivated by the smooth curve of her waist, her hip, the way that black lace underwear had barely covered her shapely rear.

But that big attraction still hadn't prepared him for what had transpired in the restaurant. She was unprac-

ticed. Much less experienc_____
judging by that kiss. She had_____

But somehow, she had lit h_____
tasted every female delicacy the w_____
lighted himself in feminine compa_____
break. Seeing no reason he could not s_____
he was bound and determined never t_____
again.

But she had broken through that jaded _____ at surrounded him. She had done something to hi__. And now, she was yelling at him.

"I could not warn you, *cara*," he said. "That would have spoiled the surprise."

"I didn't like the surprise," she said.

"Still, I needed you to look surprised. You are aware that most women do not know when they're going to be proposed to, are you not?"

She sniffed audibly. "Maybe I'm not."

"I think you are. I needed it to look real."

"Is that why you…pawed at me afterward?"

"That's a very elegant way to describe what transpired between us. Though I do believe, you did some pawing of your own."

She huffed. "I did not. Like I said, you surprised me. I feel as though you could have warned me. About all of it. And you would not have lost the element of surprise. I could have acted."

"Sadly, you're a terrible actress. I hate to be insulting, but it's true. You have no artifice." As he said it, he realized how very true it was.

"You were trying to control me," she said, her tone hard, the anger behind it indicative of a deeper wound. One that had existed long before he'd arrived in her life.

"That wasn't it," he said, although he imagined it was

point. "You have no… You're very soft.
to have no way of protecting yourself from any
at all. You sit in sunbeams with bowls of cereal.
And I do not know what to do with you. I do not know
what you might do next. I do not like it."

She breathed in deeply, and if a breath could be called
triumphant, then this one certainly was. "Good. I don't live
my life to please people anymore. I am my own person."

"Yes. So you've said."

"It's the truth. I know that I told you my parents were
difficult. But you have no idea."

"Well, you have met my parents. Assume I have some
idea of difficult parents."

She snorted. "Trust me. Your parents seemed delightful to me."

"Your frame of reference is off."

"Undoubtedly." He began to pace the length of the
room, all of the unquenched fire and unspent energy inside him threatening to boil over. "You must remember that
you are not in charge here. This thing that we're doing is
important only to me. Therefore, I will direct all actions.
If I decided that this was the best way to go about con-
firming our engagement for the public, then you must accept that my way is law."

"You keep saying this is only important to you. But
that isn't the case. I care. You may not understand it—I
don't even understand it. But it matters. I'm linked to it.
Physically. I know that these babies aren't mine, but it's
all jumbled up. Biology and ownership, what it means…
I don't know. I just know that I don't feel like a womb for
rent. I feel like a person, a person who is going through
something big and terrifying. A person who is carrying
a baby. *Babies*, even. There is no divorcing my emotions
from it. There is no detaching myself, not completely."

He regarded her closely. "Have you changed your mind about leaving?" She would. He would make sure of it. But if she was leaning toward a change of heart now, that would make his job all the easier.

Her reaction to that kiss would seal things completely.

"No," she said, her tone muted. She looked away, biting that lush lower lip that he had tasted less than an hour ago. "I can't. I have too much to do. I know that…I know that. But stop telling me that what I want doesn't matter. That what I feel isn't like what you feel."

"But," he said, unable to let that comment slide, even if he should for the sake of harmony. For the sake of manipulation. "It is the truth. I'm going to be a father to these babies. To these children. I'm going to be the one who raises them. I know what that entails. It is going to require sacrifice. Change." Until he spoke those words he had not realized that he intended to change it all. Somewhere in the back of his mind he had imagined that he would throw the raising of these children over to nannies. But now, he realized that was not the case.

He thought of his daughter. The daughter whose name he could barely stand to think, even after all these years. The daughter he sometimes saw across the room, through crowds of people, growing from a child into a young woman. Without him. Without ever knowing.

The idea of being a distant father again, even if his children were in the nursery and he was downstairs seeing to his routine while they were cared for by others, was too much.

"My life will change." He reiterated that, as much for himself as for her.

"I have a feeling mine will, too."

"Yes. Because of all the money that I will pay you."

"No," she said, her tone fierce now. "Because I was

naive. Because I was foolish to think that I could do this and feel nothing. That I could do this and simply walk away with a check at the end. This experience is never going to go away. I… I'm going to be changed," she said, sounding sad now, broken. "I thought that everything would be fine because I was committed to having this life or I didn't have ties and strings and any of those things that I was trying to avoid. But that's not true. Everything has consequences." She laughed. "I think I pushed that out of my mind. Because it was something that my father used to talk about. Consequences for actions. How everything you do will come back to you. How distressing to find out that not everything my parents taught me is wrong."

"That is usually the case," he said, her words hitting him in an uncomfortable place yet again. "Tragic though it may seem, no matter how difficult the situation, no matter how unreasonable your parents can be at times, they are often not entirely incorrect."

She shook her head. "I'm going to bed."

She turned away from him, and he reached out, grabbing hold of her arm and stopping her from going. "Remember," he said, not quite sure what he was going to say. For a moment, he just stood there holding on to her, not certain of why he had prevented her from leaving. "Remember that we have to go to New York in two weeks. If you thought tonight was public, then what you encounter there will surprise you. If you need any kind of preparation in advance, I suggest you speak to me about it. Otherwise, I will assume that you know what you're getting yourself into and I will expect you to behave accordingly."

He released his hold on her. He knew he was being an ass, but he couldn't quite bring himself to correct the behavior. Why should he?

*Seduction, perhaps?*

He gritted his teeth. Yes, that might have been the better path. To kiss her again, to soften her fears while he claimed that soft mouth of hers. And yet, he found he needed more distance from that initial kiss than another. More than he would like to admit.

"I think I can figure it out," she said, her tone soft.

"See that you do."

There were only a couple of weeks left until he would present her to the world as his fiancée. And at that point—his father was correct—it needed to be permanent. But Esther was hungry for experience. To see the world, to see all that life had to offer. And if there was anything that he possessed, it was access to what she craved.

He could give her glamour. He could give her excitement. He could—quite literally—show her the world.

And there was one more thing. Yet another that she would get from no other man, not in the way that he could give it. Passion. The two of them were combustible, there was no denying that after the kiss they had shared tonight. It was not a common kind of chemistry. He was a connoisseur of such things, and he should know.

Yes. New York would be the perfect place to spring his trap.

He would take her to the finest hotel, show her the finest art, take her to unsurpassed restaurants. And then when he took her back to that plush hotel and laid her on that big bed... He would make her his.

In the weeks since their engagement, they had settled into an odd sort of routine. They ate meals together—and she had none of them on the floor—and they shared polite conversation where he never once tried to kiss her.

He was interesting, and that was perplexing, because

she found herself seeking him out in the evenings just so she could talk to him.

Then there were the books. Every day after work he brought her a new one. Small, hardbound travel guides. Paperback novels. Extremely strange history books that focused on odd subjects such as uniforms for different armies and the types of women's clothing through the ages.

She'd asked him why, and he'd responded that it was so she could learn all the things she didn't know. Just as she'd said she wanted to.

It made her feel…soft. She wasn't sure she wanted that. She also wanted things to stay the same. In this strange, quiet lull where she felt like they were poised on the brink of something.

She liked being on the brink. It felt safe. Nothing too big, or too outside her experience.

Of course, it had to end. And she got her big shove over the brink when he came home from his office one day and swept her and all of her clothing up in a whirlwind of commands, packed her into his car and then summarily unpacked her on his private plane.

A private plane. Now, that she had not managed to imagine with any kind of accuracy. The horrors of traveling economy over the Atlantic had been something she hadn't quite anticipated, but on the opposite end of the spectrum.

The long flight to New York seemed to pass quickly with her enveloped in the butter-soft leather of the recliner in the living area of Renzo's plane. There was food that bore absolutely no resemblance to the meal she had been served on her crossing from the United States, and all manner of fresh juice and sparkling water.

Then, there was some kind of light, sweet cream cake that she could have eaten her weight in if she hadn't been stopped by the landing preparation.

Renzo had spent the entire flight buried in work. That was neither completely surprising nor unwelcome. At least, it shouldn't have been unwelcome. Except she had craved conversation but had instead settled for reading the book he'd gotten her for the flight, which strangely felt like him talking to her in some way.

She didn't know why she was being weird about it. They were connected by the babies she was carrying, and that was it. They didn't need to form more of a personal connection than they already had. More than that, it was probably best if they didn't.

She did her best not to think about that kiss. She did her best not to think of it as she was ushered off the plane and into another limousine. She did her best not to think of it as they made their way down the freeway, the famous Manhattan skyline coming into view.

That helped take her focus off Renzo and the strange ache in her chest.

New York. She had never been to New York. She had hoped to make it there someday, but her first inclination had been to get as far away from her parents as she possibly could, and that had meant taking a little sojourn around Europe.

But this was amazing. The kind of amazing that she hadn't imagined she would experience in her lifetime. At least, not when you combined it with the flight over. In some ways it was a relief to see that Renzo was making good on his promise. To show her a part of the world that she couldn't have seen without him. The way that people with money lived. The way that they traveled, the sorts of sights and foods that they saw and ate.

In another way, it was disquieting.

Because it was just another way Renzo might have

changed her. What if she got used to this? What if she missed it? She didn't want that.

She shook that thought off immediately as the city drew closer.

This was what mattered. The experience. Not the lushness of the car. But where she was. She wasn't going to change in that regard. Not that much. She had been sort of distressed when she had realized fully that her parents might have had some points when they'd lectured her about consequences.

And what she had already known was that the way they had instilled the lack of materialism in her really had mattered. It really had made a difference. And it made it a lot easier for her to pick up and travel around. While a lot of her various roommates in the different hostels had been dismayed by conditions, she had been grateful for a space of her own.

Independence was the luxury. She would remember that.

She and Renzo completed the ride down into Manhattan in silence. She remained silent all through their arrival at the hotel. It was incredible, with broad stone steps leading up to the entry. The lobby was tiled in a caramel-color stone, shot through with veins of deeper gold. It wasn't a large room. In fact, the hotel itself had a small, exclusive quality to it. But it was made to feel even more special as a result.

As though only a handful of people could ever hope to experience it.

The room, however, that had been reserved for herself and Renzo was not small. It took up the entire top of the building, bedrooms on one end and a large common living area in the center. The windows looked out over Central Park, and she stood there transfixed, gazing at the green square surrounded by all of the man-made grit and gray.

"This is amazing," she said, turning back to face him, her throat constricting when she saw him.

He was standing there, deft fingers loosening the knot on his black tie. He pulled it through his shirt collar, then undid the top button. And she found herself more transfixed by the view before her than by the one that was now behind her.

The city. She was supposed to be focusing on the city. On the hotel. On the fact that it was a new experience. She was not supposed to be obsessing on the man before her. She was not supposed to be transfixed by the strong, bronzed column of his throat. By the wedge of golden skin he revealed when he undid that top button. And not just skin. Hair. Dark chest hair that was just barely visible and captured her imagination in a way that stunned her.

It was just very male. And she knew from experience that so was he. His kiss had been like that. Very like a man. So different to her. Conquering, hard. While she had softened, yielded.

No. She would not think about that. She wouldn't think about yielding to him.

"What do you think of your first sight of New York?"

"Amazing," she said, grateful that he was asking about the city and not about his chest. "Like I said. It's big and busy like London, but different, too. The energy is different."

He frowned slightly, tilting his head to the side. "The energy is different." He nodded slowly. "I suppose that's true. Though, I had never thought of it quite that way."

"Well, you've never sat on the floor and eaten your cereal in a sunbeam either."

"Correct."

"Noticing energy is more the sort of thing someone who'd eat their cereal on the floor in a sunbeam would do."

"I would imagine that's true."

"You're too busy to notice things like that. The real estate development business is...busy, I guess."

"Yes. Even during slow times in the economy, it's comparably busy if you've already got a massive empire."

"And you do," she said.

"I would think that was obvious by now."

"Yes. Pretty obvious." She forced herself to turn away from him, forced herself to look back at the view again. "I find cities so very interesting. The anonymity of them. You can be surrounded by people and still be completely alone. Where I grew up, there were less people. By far there were less people. But it felt like you were never alone. And not just because I lived in the house with so many other people. But because every time you stepped outside you would meet somebody you knew. You could never just have a bad day."

He lifted a shoulder. "I am rarely anonymous when I go out."

She frowned. "I suppose you aren't. I mean, I would never have known who you were. I'm not metropolitan enough."

"You're certainly working on it."

She looked down at the outfit that had been chosen for her to travel in. Dark jeans and a white top. She supposed she looked much more metropolitan than she had only a few weeks ago. But it wasn't her. And none of this belonged to her either.

"The appearance of it at least." She regarded him more closely. "I suppose you can't exactly have a public bad day either."

He chuckled, the sound dark, rolling over her like a

thick summer night. "Of course I can. I can do whatever I like, behave as badly as I like. I'm Renzo Valenti, and no one is going to lecture me on decorum."

"Except maybe your mother."

He laughed again. "Oh, yes, she most definitely would. But there is nothing my parents can do to me." He looked past her, at the city visible through the large windows. "They gave me too much freedom for too long, and now I have too much power. All they can do is direct their disapproval at me with as much fervor as humanly possible. A pity for them, but rather a win for me, don't you think?"

"In some ways approval and disapproval is power, isn't it?" She thought of her own family. Of the fact that what had kept her rooted in her childhood home for so long was the knowledge that if she should ever leave she would never be able to go back. That if she ever stepped foot out of line her father would disown her. Would turn all of her siblings against her, would forbid her mother from having any contact with her. It was the knowledge that the disapproval would carry so much weight she would be cut off completely, and in order to make even one decision of her own she would have to be willing to accept that as a consequence.

"I suppose."

"You don't believe me. But that just means that your parents' approval doesn't come with strings."

That made him laugh again, and he wandered over to the bar, taking out a bottle of Scotch and pouring himself a drink. She wouldn't have known what the amber-colored alcohol was only a few months ago, but waiting tables had educated her.

"Now, that isn't true. It's only that I possess a certain amount of string-pulling power myself. So what you have is a power struggle more than a fait accompli."

"That's what I needed," she said, "strings."

Of course, that was what actually hurt, she concluded, standing there and turning over what he said. The fact that she wasn't a string. Her presence in their life wasn't a string. Control mattered to her father, not love. And he couldn't have anyone around to challenge that control because it might inspire the other people in his household to do the same.

Parental love wasn't strong enough to combat that. If there was any parental love coming from his direction at all.

"You should probably get some rest. You will have to start getting ready for the gala tonight as soon as possible. So a short nap might be in your best interest."

She wasn't exactly sure what had inspired the abrupt comment, but she would be grateful for some distance. Grateful for a little bit of time away from Renzo and his magnetic presence, and all of the feelings and emotions he stirred up inside her.

"I think I will have a nap. Is… Is someone going to come and help with my makeup and hair?"

"Of course. I'm hardly going to leave that to chance on the night of the most important professional event of the year."

"Good. I'm too relieved to be offended." And then she turned and walked away from him, heading into the first bedroom that she saw. Without another thought, she threw herself across the plush mattress and closed her eyes.

And if it was Renzo she saw behind her closed lids rather than the brilliant city skyline, she chose to ignore that.

Renzo had a plan. And he had a feeling it would be one that was quite simple to complete. He was intent on seducing Esther tonight. Judging by the way she had looked at him this afternoon, the seduction was halfway complete. He was not a vain man, but he was also not a man given to false modesty.

Esther was attracted to him. She had been affected by that kiss, and he would be able to overtake her senses yet again when he touched her tonight. More than that, she was affected by all of this. By the luxury of the travel, by the places in the world that he brought to her fingertips by virtue of his money and connections.

He wasn't angry that she had an interest in these things; rather, he found it to be a boon to his cause.

If she had been as unaffected by these things as she had claimed that she would be, then he would have lost some leverage. But she wanted to go to school, she wanted to see the world, and whether she knew it or not, she craved his touch. He could give her all of those things. He could satisfy her in a way that no other man could, in a way no other man had.

All she would have to do was agree to marry him. Beyond that, she would have to present a respectable front in public. But that was it. He could see no reason she would find that objectionable.

He had lied to her, of course, when he said that his parents had no leverage with him. His father had presented incredibly hard leverage at his home only two weeks ago. And dammit all, Renzo was not immune. He would not have control in his stake of the family business given up to his brother-in-law. He would not have it given to anyone. He had given up enough.

In order to maintain the status quo, he had already given up a child. He would not lose anything more.

Rage burned in his chest, the kind of rage he had not felt for years. He hadn't realized it was quite so strong still. He had thought he had accepted that decision. His parents had been acting in his best interest. But it burned. In fact, the more the years passed, it seemed to burn even brighter.

The older he got, the more control he assumed of his life, the angrier he was about the lack of control he'd had at sixteen.

His line of thinking was cut off completely when the door to Esther's room opened and a flash of slender leg caught his gaze. He turned his focus to her, a hot slug of lead landing in his gut and making his body feel heavy.

Her dark hair was hanging loose, in glossy waves around her shoulders. The bright blue dress she had in place showed off her curves, enhancing her modest bust with the heart-shaped line.

The shimmering, fluttering fabric hung loose over her stomach, a stomach that was showing subtle changes brought about by the pregnancy.

Gold shadow enhanced her eyes, and her cheeks were the color of poppies, matching her full lips.

She was an explosion of color, of shimmering light, and he could not take his eyes off her. Not for the first time, he wondered who might be seducing whom. Perhaps the idea of staying with him was in her plans already. Perhaps all of this was an elaborate ruse to gain access to his wealth and power.

Looking at her now, combined with the incontrovertible evidence of her pregnancy from the scan, he wasn't sure if it mattered. If she was every bit as innocent as she claimed, and appeared to be, or if she was calculating.

He should care. He just found that he didn't.

"You look amazing," he said, closing the space between them and curving his arm around her waist. The stylist he had hired was behind her in the room, and he knew that he could use that as an excuse later for what he was about to do.

He leaned in, brushing his lips against hers. A taste, a tease for them both.

It became apparent immediately that he had not imagined the heat and fire between them. In fact, just that brief touch ignited something inside him that was hotter than anything he'd felt in his memory.

It was nothing. Just lips. Just a hand on the curve of her waist.

And it left him shaken.

"Come," he said, his voice rough, "*cara*, let us go to the ball."

# CHAPTER NINE

THE VENUE WAS packed full of people, lavish and expensive, money dripping from every corner of the place. From the diamonds that hung in women's ears, to the chandelier that hung overhead. It was the perfect example of the kind of opulent lifestyle that Renzo could offer her if she chose to stay with him. The perfect piece of manipulation, and one he had not even planned for.

But it would do. It would do nicely. Esther clung to his side, her delicate fingers curved around his biceps. And even though there were layers between them—his coat and his shirt—he could still feel the heat from her skin.

Yes, this was a very nice diversion, and one that would work to his advantage, but he couldn't wait till after. Till he would finally strip her bare and hold her in his arms. It had become a madness over the past few weeks. To resist her, to wait.

To speak to her over dinner when he'd wanted to pull her over the table and have her there. To bring her books to read in bed, when he wanted to keep her occupied with other things in bed.

He had thought so many times of going into her room and breaking the door down, laying his body over hers and kissing her until neither of them could breathe.

Of taking full possession of her without any of this

pretense. Without any of this delicacy. Because he had a feeling that it wasn't needed. He had a feeling that the fire burned as hot in her as it did in him. And he desperately wanted to find out if that was true.

However, he could not afford to allow impetuousness to make his decisions for him. He could not afford to make a wrong move simply because his libido was ratcheted up several notches.

He shifted, her hip brushing against him. The reaction was immediate. Primal.

He wanted to hold on to those hips, hold her steady as he thrust into her. As he made her cry out. Thankfully, he had thought to call the doctor before they left Rome. Under the guise of discussing safe travel. And he had of course asked her about what sort of intimacy would be all right, given that the pregnancy was considered a slightly higher risk.

She said that normal intercourse would be fine.

A smile curved his lips. Yes, he was going to have her. Tonight.

"There are so many people here," Esther said, "and they all seem to know you."

"Yes, but I do not know them."

"What must that be like?" she asked, as though he hadn't spoken. "To be…famous."

"*Infamous*, more like. I'm not going to lie to you, I'm mostly well-known because men know they have to watch their women around me." Now she stiffened, and he was pleased with himself for that well-timed comment. It was a risk, but there was no hiding his reputation from her. However, using it to fire up a little jealousy in her couldn't hurt, certainly.

"Is that so?" she asked.

"Yes," he said. "I was single for a very long time, Esther. And I didn't see any point in living with restraint. As I told you earlier, I don't have to watch the way that I behave. I have a certain amount of immunity granted to me because I am both male and very rich."

"That must be nice."

"I don't know any differently."

"My father was big on the men-having-whatever-they-wanted thing," she said, the tone of her voice disinterested, casual, but he sensed something deep beneath the surface.

"Traditional, was he?"

She shook her head. "I don't know. Maybe that's one word for it. One of the things I've been working on is recognizing that whatever my father and the other men like him believed, it isn't necessarily connected to anything real. It's not about other people who believe similarly to them. They took something that was all right and twisted it to suit their own ends. And I do understand that."

"You had…a religious upbringing?"

She shrugged. "I'm hesitant to call it that. I'm not going to put the blame on religion. Just the people involved."

"Very progressive of you."

She shrugged both shoulders this time. "Isn't that the point of life? To progress? That's what I'm trying to do. Move forward. Not live underneath the cloud of all of that." She looked up, refracted light shimmering across her face from the chandelier above them as she did. "I'm not under a cloud at all right now." She smiled then, and all of the thoughts he had earlier about her potentially calculated behavior faded. It was difficult for him to imagine somebody who was simply genuine. Because it was outside his experience. Yet, Esther seemed to be, and if he looked at her from that angle, if you looked at her now, he felt slightly guilty about what he intended to do. Because that really did make it a manipulation, rather than a simple seduction.

But still, she would get everything that she wanted in the end, just in a slightly different format. So, he should not feel guilt.

He turned, and suddenly it felt as though the chandelier had detached from the ceiling and come crashing down around him. It was everything he'd been afraid of, and yet no amount of forward thinking could ever prepare him for it.

There she was.

Samantha.

His daughter.

Seeing her like this, closer to being a woman than a girl, always shocked him. But then, everything about this had always been shocking, horrifying. Seeing her was always something like having his guts torn out straight through his stomach. Having his heart pulled out of his mouth.

It was a pain that never healed, and for a man who avoided strong emotion at all cost it was anathema. He controlled the world. He controlled more money than most people could fathom. He had more—would have more—than many small countries ever would. And yet he did not have her, and there was nothing he could do about it. Nothing he could do short of destroying what she thought her life was. Who she thought she was.

In this, he was helpless. And he despised it.

But there was very little that could be done. In order to be a good man in this situation, in order to be a controlled man, he had to go against everything his instincts told him to do. He had to honor the life that he had chosen to give to his daughter. Even if he had been coerced into it, the ultimate result was the same. There were things she believed about herself and her parents that he could not shake, not now.

He knew it. He knew it, but he despised it.

Fire burned inside him, rage, intensity. He couldn't go to her. All he could do was hold even more tightly to Esther. And as he did, he held even more tightly to his conviction. He had to make her his. At all costs. Because he would never take a chance that he might lose his children, not again.

He had lost one daughter. And the pain never faded. He doubted it ever would. There was nothing that could be done about it. It was a red slash across his life that could never heal. A mistake that would not be undone.

Oh, her existence wasn't a mistake. It never could be. The mixture of grief and pride that filled him when he saw Samantha was something that defied description. It was all-encompassing, overwhelming. She was not a mistake. She was destined for a life that was better than the one he could have given her at the time. Than the one she would have had if she had been raised by an angry, bitter woman whose marriage was destroyed because of her existence and a sixteen-year-old boy who could scarcely take care of himself, let alone a little girl.

Yes, there was no doubt she was living a better life than he could have given at the time.

But now… Now he had no excuses. Now he had resources, he had experience, maturity. He had already lived an entire existence trying to prove that he was unsuitable to raise the child he'd had at far too young an age.

Now he was going to have to fashion a new existence. One where he became everything these children would need.

He would give them everything. Starting with a family. One with no room for Ashley, who had engineered their existence for the sole purpose of manipulating him. One that consisted of a mother and a father. Esther. She was the one. She was going to give birth to them. She was the one the public would consider theirs, and so, too, would they.

He was renewed in his purpose. As he stood there, his insides being torn to shreds piece by piece as he looked at the beautiful young woman whom he would never know, who shared his DNA but would always remain a stranger, his purpose was renewed.

He turned away from Samantha. He turned back to Esther. "Dance with me," he said.

She blinked. "I don't know how to dance."

"Don't tell me, dancing was forbidden?"

She laughed, but the sound was uncomfortable, and it made him feel guilty. "Yes," she said. "Dancing was definitely something that was off the table. But...I did a lot of things I wasn't supposed to."

Something about that admission made his stomach tight, made his blood run hotter. "Is that right?"

"Yes," she said, her cheeks turning pink. "But I didn't dance. I might embarrass you."

"You're the most beautiful woman in the room. Even if you step all over my feet I will not be embarrassed to be seen with you."

A warm flush of color spread up her cheeks, her dark eyes bright. She liked that. This attention, the compliments. He reached out, sliding his thumb over her cheekbone, tracing that wash of color that had appeared there. "Do you know that you're beautiful?"

"It's nothing that I ever gave much thought to. I mean, I've probably given it much more thought ever since I met you."

He drew her close to him, guiding her to the dance floor, curving his arm around her waist and taking her hand in his. "In a good way, I hope?"

She looked down. "Meeting you has made me think a lot about people."

"I'm not sure I follow you."

She moved easily along with him as he guided her in time with the music. But she kept her eyes downcast. "Just…people. Men, women." She looked up then, something open and naked in her gaze. It held him fast, hit him square in the chest. "How different we are. What it means. Why it matters. My beauty never mattered until I wanted you to see it. And then, well, since then I've wondered about it. If I had it, and if I did, if it was the kind that you noticed. It's a weird way to think about it, maybe. But I never spent much of my life thinking about how I looked except in the context that being vain about it was wrong." She shook her head, her dark hair rippling over her shoulders. "That's quite liberating in a way. If vanity is wrong, then you simply push thoughts of your appearance out of your mind. You don't worry about it, and neither does anyone around you. But that isn't the way the rest of the world works."

"Sadly not."

"I guess that's another thing about how I was raised that maybe isn't so bad. Because now I have worried about it. How my dresses fit, how they look, what you think. But then… Feeling beautiful isn't so bad. And when you tell me that I am…"

"You like it," he said.

"I do."

His stomach tightened, and a smile curved his lips, a feeling of anticipation lancing him. He was very close to having her in the palm of his hand. To having all that glorious skin under his hands. "Vain creature," he said, injecting a note of levity into his voice.

"Is that a bad thing?" she asked, her tone tentative.

"I find it somewhat charming. Though, I have to ask you now… What have you been thinking about me? You said you had been thinking about our differences."

The undertone of pink in her cheeks turned scarlet. "That's silly. Juvenile. You don't want to hear about that."

"Oh, I assure you I do."

He examined the lush curve of her mouth, the dramatic high cheekbones and her dark lashes. She was the epitome of glorious feminine beauty, but there was an innocence there, and part of him wondered just how much.

"You're just very…" Her lashes fluttered "…big. I'm small. I feel like you could overpower me if you wanted to, and yet, you never have. There's something incredibly powerful about that. It feels dangerous to be near you sometimes, and yet I know you won't hurt me. I don't how to describe that. But sometimes the realization washes over me and it makes me shiver."

He did something then that he could not quite fully reason out. He released his hold on her hand, sliding his fingertips up her arm and resting his thumb against the hollow at the base of her throat as he curved his fingers around the back of her neck. Demonstrating that power, perhaps.

He could feel her pulse beginning to throb faster beneath his touch, and he felt an answering pounding within his own body.

"What else?" he asked, keeping his tone soft and his touch firm.

"You're very…hard."

"Am I?" he asked, lowering his voice further.

She had no idea. He was getting harder by the second. This little flirtation, something he hadn't quite anticipated enjoying, was adding fuel to the fire of his determination.

"Yes," she said, doing something completely unexpected, taking her free hand and pressing it against his chest, sliding her palm down to his stomach. "Much harder than I am."

"You seem like you would benefit from the chance to explore that."

Her breath caught in her throat. "I don't…"

He reached down, catching hold of her wrist and pressing her hand more firmly against his chest. "I want you."

He wanted her. Needed her. And not just because he needed her to marry him, because he needed to ensure that she was bound to him. But because he needed something to blot out the unending pain that was coursing through him—had been coursing through him for sixteen years.

Her eyes widened, an innocent stain spreading across her cheeks. "Want me to…what?"

He pulled her even closer, pressing his lips against her ear. "I want you naked," he said, feeling her shiver against him. "I want to lay you down in my bed and strip that dress from your body. Then I want to touch every inch of you. And then I want to taste you."

He barely recognized his own voice. It was rough, hard. And he was somewhere past control.

Esther trembled, and he could feel her shaking her head. "No, you don't."

"Of course I do. I said you were beautiful. I meant it."

"But that doesn't mean…" Her cheeks looked like they were on fire beneath her golden skin. "There are plenty of other women you could have. You don't have an obligation to me. We might be engaged publicly, but we both know that privately…"

"Of course I can be seen with no other woman but you," he said, "but that is beside the point. You're the one that I want. You, Esther Abbott. Not anyone else."

"But I'm not…I don't know… You can't. Not me."

The fire in him burned even hotter, and he was surprised by the strength of his conviction. Yes, it was all tangled up in the need to keep possession of his children, the need to give them the best life possible, and he believed he needed Esther for that, but there was more. In this moment, there was more. It would not be a hardship to convince her that he wanted her. Because he did.

"Yes," he returned, "you. I love your skin. I want to know if it's smooth like this all over." He moved a fingertip over her arm, relishing the tremor that racked her frame. "Your lips." He moved his fingertip around the lush line of her mouth then, that softness doing something to all of the hard, jagged places inside him. The seduction working better on him than he had intended. This was supposed to be about an end goal, one that extended far beyond finding himself between her beautiful thighs tonight. But it was difficult to remember that with lust pounding through him like a drumbeat.

"Your hands," he said, moving to curve his fingers around her wrist, caressing her palm slowly. "I want to feel them all over my body. And yes, I could have another woman. I have had them. More than I can count, I won't lie to you. But I don't want them now. I couldn't." It was the truth in his words that surprised him more than anything else. The fact that this wasn't simply a calculated statement. The fact that the strange creature in front of him had bewitched him in some way.

That she had compelled him to give her books, of all the ridiculous things. A new one every day because he passed a shop on his way home from work, and he thought of her every time he did. Because she wanted to learn and he wanted her to.

And, *Dio*, what he would teach her tonight.

"You haunt me," he ground out, losing hold of the carefully scripted line of compliments that he had put together moments before, going off into the dark parts of himself, where he could scarcely see an inch in front of him, much less guess at what might come out of his mouth next. "My dreams," he said, the words rough, "and every moment I lay in bed not dreaming because I'm thinking about you."

Her entire body was shaking like a leaf in a storm, and he felt nothing but triumph. His vision was a blur, a haze of everything but Esther. His mind blank of everything except what would happen in the moments immediately following this one.

She would say yes. She had to.

She pulled away slightly, and he wondered if he had gone too far. If he had been too intense, if he had been too honest.

He made a decision then.

He took firm hold of her arms and dragged her forward, closing the distance between them and claiming her mouth with his own. He wrapped her up in him then, folding her in his arms, gripping her chin tightly as he braced her firmly against him and forged a new, intimate territory between them.

He had kissed her before. But not like this. This wasn't a show for the people around them. It was not designed for cameras. And it wasn't designed to end here.

It was a beginning. A promise. A precursor of what was to come. An echo of the act that he intended to follow.

As he thrust his tongue in and out of the sweet, hot depths, as he felt her moan and shake beneath him, he knew that he had won. Because if he could reduce her to this—reduce them both to this—here in the presence of all these other people, then there would be no resisting him once he had her alone.

His father would be angry. Because Renzo had not taken this opportunity to forge new business deals as he had promised. But his father had no idea about the other war that was being raged. The war to keep Esther close, the war to defend the family that was growing inside her even now.

It took all the strength that he possessed to pull away from her. To keep himself from pushing her into the nearest alcove, shoving her dress up her hips and taking her then and there. Claiming her. But that would only further the cause of satisfying his desire. It would not further the cause of seduction.

He doubted if Esther had ever been taken up against a wall in a public place. And he also doubted if she would find that overly romantic.

As much as his body didn't care, the rest of him had to. He managed to find his focus in that. And when he turned back around and saw his daughter standing at the back of the room chatting with friends and taking no notice of what had been happening with him—why would she? She had no idea who he even was—it brought him crashing down to reality with an extreme sense of purpose.

"Come," he said.

She blinked. "We haven't been here that long. We came all the way to New York for this."

He laughed, every jagged thing inside him brought to the surface because of what had happened tonight stabbing through him. "No, *cara*. I came all the way to New York for you. To seduce you. To have you."

She looked shaken by that, her dark eyes filled with confusion. "You could have had me in Rome," she said finally, her tone muted.

"But I will have you here," he said, smoothing his thumb over her swollen lower lip. "With this city in the background, on that big bed in a beautiful hotel. In this place that you've never been before, where no other man has ever had you. And I swear to you, you will never forget it."

She looked away from him, hesitating for a moment as though she were about to say something. But then, she didn't. Instead, she simply nodded and took his hand.

# CHAPTER TEN

THERE WAS A wild thing inside Esther. She had always been afraid of it. From the moment she had first suspected that it was there. Of course, it was that very wild thing that had inspired her to rebel against her family in the first place. That had inspired her to break the strict code she'd been raised in to seek out other things.

That had gotten her thrown out of the only home she'd ever known.

But even when she'd left, she'd hoped to control it in some way. Had never imagined she would give it free rein.

She had told herself that she wasn't going to find a man, because she needed freedom. She had told herself she didn't care about making herself look more beautiful, because she had a world to see, and who cared what it saw when it looked back at her.

But there was more to it than that. This was what she had always been afraid of. That the moment she met a beautiful man, the moment that he touched her, she would be lost. Because that wild thing inside her wasn't simply hungry for the beauty of the world, wasn't simply hungry for a taste of food.

It was hungry for the carnal things. For the sensual things. For the touch of a man's hands on her bare skin.

For the hot press of his lips against hers, and on her neck, and down lower.

Renzo had ripped the cover off all her pretense. He had exposed her. Not to him—she had a feeling she had been exposed to him from the moment she'd seen him. It was the fact he had exposed her so effectively to herself that had her shaken.

But she wasn't turning back. Not now. There was no way. Not now that she knew. Not now that she wanted. With such a sharp keenness that it could not be denied.

She didn't want to deny it.

There was a conversation they would have to have. After this. They would have it after. She didn't want to say anything that would make him stop now. She had a feeling that he had some suspicions about her lack of experience, but what he had said just a few moments earlier about having her in the city where no other man had ever been with her before made her think that he perhaps didn't know just how inexperienced she was.

That he hadn't guessed yet that he was the first man to kiss her. That he would most certainly be the first man to...

She shivered as the limousine pulled up in front of the hotel. She could tell him no. She knew she could. And he would stop.

She thought back to the fierce way he had taken her mouth in that room full of people. It had been something more than a kiss, something so intimate it made her catch fire inside to think about other people seeing it.

He had been beyond himself then, all of that icy control that she had witnessed in him from the first time she'd seen him burned away. Scorched by the fire of the attraction between them.

She swallowed hard, looking over at him, at the hard carved lines of his face that seemed to look even more intimidating now than they ever had. She was fairly certain that he would stop if she asked him to.

Yes, of course he would. He was a man, not a monster. Even if he was a man she could scarcely recognize now. There was an intensity to him that she had never witnessed before. A desperation, a hunger. It mirrored her own and stoked the flames inside her so that they burned brighter, hotter.

He didn't touch her during the elevator ride up to the penthouse. She was afraid, for a moment, that it might give her too much time to think. That it might allow the heated passion inside her to begin to cool.

But once the doors closed behind them and they were ensconced in the tight space, she found it to be entirely the opposite. She could scarcely breathe for wanting him. For needing him.

The seconds in the elevator stretched between them tight and thick, wrapping around her neck, constricting her throat. By the time the doors opened into the hall, she let out a great gasp, a sigh of relief that she knew he had heard.

He still didn't touch her as they approached the door and he used the key card to undo the lock. But then he placed his palm on her lower back, ushering her in, the contact burning through the thin fabric of her dress.

And when he closed the door behind them, she was the one who closed the remaining distance between them. She was the one to kiss him. Because she didn't want him to change his mind. Didn't want whatever madness he was beholden to to fade. She kissed him with all of that desperation. That need for satisfaction.

She began to frantically work at the knot on his tie, clumsy fingers then moving to the buttons on his shirt.

"Slow down," he said, his voice a low, gravelly command.

"No," she said, between kisses, between desperate grabs for his shirt fabric. "No," she said again, "I can't."

He reached up, taking hold of her wrists, his hold on her like irons. "There is no rush," he said, leaning in slowly, brushing his cheek against hers. It was much more innocuous contact than the kiss from before, and yet it affected her no less profoundly. "Some things are best when they're taken slowly."

Taken slowly? She felt like there was a wild creature inside her trying to break out, desperate for release, and he wanted to talk about taking it slowly? She had waited twenty-three years for this moment. To be with a man. To want a man like this. And now, with satisfaction so close, he wanted to take it slowly.

She wanted it done now.

That certainty surprised her, especially after the small attack of nerves that she'd had right before coming into the hotel. There were no nerves now, not in here.

What she said to him out on the dance floor, it had been true. His strength, the way that he kept it leashed, all the while with her totally conscious of how easily he could overpower her, was a powerful aphrodisiac.

"I don't want slow," she said, leaning back into him.

And now, he used that strength against her, holding her fast, not allowing her to kiss him again. "Wait," he said, his tone firm.

He shifted his hold, gathering both of her wrists into one hand, then lowering his free hand to her back, grabbing hold of her dress's zipper tab and pulling it down slowly. The filmy fabric fell away from her curves, leaving her standing there in nothing more than a pair of lace panties.

It was similar to what had happened that day he'd come to her fitting. But also, like something completely different. She had been facing away from him then, and though she had been able to feel his eyes on her, she had not seen the expression on his face. She could see it now.

All of that lean hunger directed at her, the intensity of a predator gleaming in those dark eyes. He looked her over slowly, making no effort to hide his appreciation for her breasts as he allowed himself a long moment to stare openly at them.

They felt heavier all of a sudden. Her nipples tightening beneath his close inspection. An answering ache started between her thighs, and she felt herself getting slicker, felt her need ratcheting up several notches without him putting a hand on her.

"See?" he asked, the knowing look in his eye borderline humiliating. "Slow is good. It will be better for you. I don't know what kind of experiences you've had before, but I can guess at the sort of men a woman traveling alone and staying in hostels meets. I can guess the sort of sex those kinds of semipublic quarters necessitate. But we have all night, and we have this room, we have a very big bed. And you have me. I am not a man who rushes his vices, *cara*. Rather, I prefer to linger over them."

"Am I a vice?" she asked, her voice trembling.

"The very best kind."

He leaned in, scraping his teeth across her chin before moving upward, kissing her mouth lightly before catching her lip in a sharp bite. The sensation hit her low and deep, unexpected and sharp, and not unpleasant at all.

He tightened his hold on her, reinforcing his control as he angled his head and kissed her neck, tracing a line down her vulnerable skin with the tip of his tongue. Her nipples grew even tighter, begging for his attention. She knew what she wanted, but she was much too embarrassed to say. She didn't even know enough to know for sure if it was a reasonable thing to want.

But, thankfully, he seemed to be able to read her mind.

He moved his attentions lower then, tracing the outline of one tightened bud before sucking her in deep, the sensation sending sparks down low in her midsection that radiated outward. She struggled against his hold, because she needed to grab on to something, rather than simply stand there helpless, with her wrists captured by him.

If he noticed, he didn't respond. If he cared, he didn't show it. Instead, he continued on his exploration of her body. Turning his attention to her other breast and repeating the motion there. She seemed to feel it everywhere, over every inch of her skin. It made everything far too sensitive, made everything far too real. And not real enough all at the same time.

Part of her felt like she was hovering above the scene, watching it happen to someone else, because this couldn't be happening to her. It was safe, though, to view it that way. Because the alternative was to exist in her skin all while feeling it was far too tight for her body.

Then, he released his hold on her, planting his hands tightly on her hips and pulling her up against him before sliding them around to her rear and letting his fingertips slip beneath the lace fabric of her panties, cupping her bare flesh.

And then she wasn't divided at all. Then, she wasn't hovering over the scene. She was in it, and everything was far too sharp, far too close. She felt too much, wanted too much. The hollow ache inside her was as intense as a knife's cut, slicing unerringly beneath her skin and releasing a hemorrhage of need.

He squeezed her, pulling her more tightly against his body, allowing her to feel the evidence of his need for her. He was so big, so hard, everything she had never known to fantasize about. And yet, it was terrifying, too, even as it was the fulfillment of her every need.

Because she didn't know what to do with this. Didn't know what to do with a man such as him. But she had a feeling she was about to find out.

Slowly, so very slowly, he pushed her panties down her legs and slipped them over her feet—still clad in the jeweled flats she'd put on earlier. Then, he knelt before her, removing her shoes as he had done that day in her room.

Only this time, when he was finished and he looked up at her, she knew that there was no barrier between her body and his gaze. She shivered, relishing being his focus, wanting to hide herself from him, as well.

He gripped hold of her legs, sliding his hands firmly up the length of them, to her thighs, where he paused in front of her, looking his fill at her exposed body. She pressed her knees tightly together, as though that would do something to hide her from him. As if it would do something to stop the pounding ache.

He looked up at her, a smile curving his lips. Instinctively, she struggled to get away from him, but he held her fast. And then he leaned in, the hot press of his lips against her hip bone making her jerk with surprise.

"Don't worry, *cara*," he said, tracing a faint line inward with the tip of his tongue. "I'm going to take care of you."

Surely this was wicked. That was the predominant thought she had when he moved unerringly to her center, his tongue hot and wet at the source of her need for him. Surely this was the height of her rebellion. The furthest that she could fall.

He tightened his hold on her, the blunt tips of his fingers digging into the soft skin on her rear as he took his sampling of her body deeper, as he slid his tongue all the way through her slick folds and back again, a rumbling sound of approval vibrating through his massive frame.

And then she simply didn't care. If it was wrong, if they were wrong. She didn't care about anything, anything at all except for the exquisite sensations he was lavishing her body with. She shivered as his tongue passed over the sensitive bundle of nerves again and again, establishing a rhythm that she thought might crack her into tiny pieces.

She planted her hands on his shoulders, and she didn't push him away. Instead, she braced herself as he stole her control with each pass of his tongue. As he worked to reduce her to a puddle of nothing more than shock and need. Oh, but the need won out. And if it was shocking, if she felt scandalized, it only made all of it that much more delicious.

Because this was the dark secret thing inside her allowed to come out and play. This was the piece of herself she had most feared, and here she was living it. She had always been afraid that she was wrong. That she could never, ever be the person her parents wanted her to be, no matter how her dad yelled at her. No matter how they tried to control her. She was proving it right. She had started on this journey more than a year ago, and this was the logical end.

But it didn't feel like a disaster. If anything, it felt like a triumph.

Suddenly, he shifted positions, taking hold of one thigh and draping it over his hip before he wrapped an arm around her waist, keeping the other firmly planted on her rear as he stood, bracing her body against his as he walked them through the main room of the penthouse toward one of the bedrooms.

She clung to his shoulders, shivering as his hot breath fanned over her flesh, as shock and anticipation continued to fire through her with a strength that seemed beyond reality.

When they came into the bedroom, he moved to the end of the bed, setting her down on the edge before going to his knees again, gripping her hips and bringing her to his mouth. He settled her legs over his shoulders, her heels pressed against his shoulder blades as he tasted her deeper, adding his fingers now, pressing one deep inside her. The unfamiliar invasion making her gasp.

But any discomfort was erased as he moved the flat of his tongue over her again and again in time with that finger, before adding a second, pushing her higher, harder than she had imagined it was possible to go. She was moving toward a goal she didn't even recognize. All she knew was need, but she didn't know what it was she needed.

He increased the pace, the pressure, and she forgot to breathe, forgot to think. She threw one arm over her eyes, moving her hips in time with him, not caring if that was wrong. Not caring if she should be embarrassed. She didn't care about anything but satisfying that need. And she knew this was it, she knew that he possessed the power to do it, and she would give him anything, allow him any liberty, in order to see it done.

Then suddenly it all broke apart, the tension that was screaming inside her bursting into shards of glass, shimmering inside her, bright and deadly and much more acute than anything she'd ever known before.

He continued to trace the shape of her with his tongue as aftershocks rolled through her, taking his time, satisfying himself even as she lay there assaulted by the shock of her own satisfaction.

"Renzo," she said, feeling unsteady, trembling all the way through. "I need…"

"I'll give you what you need," he said. "Patience."

She didn't even know what she needed. She shouldn't need anything more than what he'd already given. And yet, she could sense that something was missing. That she wouldn't be fully satisfied until she had him—all of him—inside her.

But then he moved away from her, standing and picking up where she had left off with his shirt, undoing each button slowly, revealing more and more golden skin, hard-packed muscles and the perfect amount of dark hair sprinkled over them.

She ached to touch him. To taste him. But she was boneless, and she found that she couldn't move. Her throat went dry as she watched his slow removal of clothing, the maddeningly methodical reveal of his body. And when his hands went to his silver belt buckle, everything in her froze.

She had never seen a naked man before. She wasn't sure if she was glad then, or if she regretted that she had no other experience to fall back on.

She licked her lips as he lowered that zipper, slowly, everything so very slow, her attention undivided. And then he pushed them down his lean hips—taking his underwear along with them—revealing every inch of his masculinity to her hungry gaze.

Her stomach clenched tight, seizing with desire and no small amount of virginal fear when she saw him.

In the back of her mind she tried to placate herself, tried to say things about new experiences and all of that. Except, it didn't work. It didn't work because he was more than just a new experience. Because she wasn't just having sex with him for the sake of experiencing sex. She wanted him. She wanted him in spite of her nerves, she wanted him more than she could ever remember wanting anything.

It was terrifying in its way. You want someone so much, in spite of any and all hints of fear or doubt. To know that it might end badly and to not care at all. It was also fascinating and about the best reason to do something that she could even think of. Because she couldn't help herself. Because she felt there was no other option.

"You don't have to worry about me. My health," he clarified. "I was extensively tested post-Ashley. And I haven't been with anyone else since."

"I'm good," she said, before she could even fully sort through what he was saying.

"Good," he said.

He joined her on the bed, placing his hand on her head and moving his palm down her thigh, then back up again, to the indent of her waist, to her breast. He cupped her, moving his thumb over her nipple. She gasped, arching against him, shocked at the ferocity with which she wanted him so soon after that soul-shattering release.

He kissed her, and as he did he settled between her thighs, the blunt head of his arousal pressing against her slick entrance. She let her head fall back, everything in her sighing *yes*. She wanted him. There was no doubt now. None at all.

And if there was fear? It was all part of it. All sacrificed on this altar. She was giving him her fear, her body, her virginity. It was what made it matter. It was what made it feel so immense. And that immensity was what made her embrace it so completely.

She would never be the same after this. Her eyes met his as the thought clicked into place, as he began to press inside her. The enormity of that filled her as he did, blotting out the brief, sharp pain that accompanied his invasion.

She reached up, touching his face, not able to tear her gaze away from him. He was... He was inside her. Part of her. They were joined together. And she knew that changed everything. She knew that—for her—there was no experiencing this on a casual level. That for her sex would always be deep like this, something that echoed inside her and resonated through to her soul.

He flexed his hips forward, and she saw stars as he moved even deeper, as he butted up against that sensitive bundle of nerves there. She clutched his shoulders as he established a steady rhythm, pushing them both to the brink, his rough, uneven breathing the soundtrack of her desire.

Knowing that he was so close to the edge, knowing that he was as affected as she was, only pushed her arousal to an even higher place. Impossible. It was impossible to think she could contain so much. So much need, so much of him. She would break apart completely if she didn't find release soon, and yet, she almost didn't want to come. Almost wanted to stay like this, poised on the brink of pain, and closer to anyone than she had ever been in her life.

She moved her hands down from his shoulders, her fingertips skimming over his muscles, feeling his strength as he braced himself above her, as he thrust into her harder and harder. She loved that. This feeling that consumed all of her, that was too much and not enough.

This was life. Life unfiltered, unprotected. Raw and intense, and no doubt every bit as dangerous as she had always been taught.

But it was real. Real in a way nothing else had ever been.

He growled, and it was that sound, that show of intensity, that sent her over the edge. Orgasm rocked her, this release going deeper, hitting her harder than the one that had come before it.

She clung to him long after the release passed, held him while he tensed, and then shattered, his muscles trembling as he gave in to his own pleasure. As powerful as it had been to find climax with him, it was his that undid her. To have him shake and shudder over her body, in her body, this man who was so much more experienced than she was, who was larger than life and seemed to be built out of stone… To have him lose his control because of her was altering in every way.

In a way it never could have been if he weren't the man he was. If he were an easy man, one who gave easily to the environment around him, then she would have simply been one more element that changed the shape of him.

Instead, this made her different. It made her matter. She had moved a mountain, and only a few hours ago she would have said that wasn't possible.

He was different from her father. Who controlled her because he was afraid of what she could be. That wasn't Renzo. It made her wonder if Renzo controlled everything around him because he was afraid of himself.

And that, she supposed, was the difference between a man who acted from a place of weakness and a man such as Renzo, who was coming from a place of damaged strength.

She didn't know why she thought that, why she imagined he was anything other than perfect and beautiful and whole as he presented himself.

Maybe it was because she had seen him in pieces just now. Just like her.

He moved away from her then, levering himself into a sitting position and pushing his hand through his dark hair. "You could have told me you were a virgin."

# CHAPTER ELEVEN

"I GENUINELY THOUGHT it was self-evident," she said, not sure how she felt that he was leading with that. "And I kind of thought that after the procedures at the fertility clinic it might not be obvious. I do think that it would be obvious given the fact that I clearly don't know how to kiss."

He shook his head. "A lot of people have sex without knowing what they're doing, Esther. A lack of skill can speak to the fact you've been with men who didn't handle you correctly."

"Well, there were none. I dropped enough hints about my childhood that… Anyway. It doesn't matter. Are you saying you wouldn't have slept with me if you'd known?"

"No," he returned, his voice rough.

"Well, then I suppose this is a fight that isn't worth having."

"I might have been a little bit gentler with you."

"All the more reason for me to not tell you. Because… I liked how you did it."

He treated her to a hard look. "You don't know better."

She shrugged, suddenly feeling small and naked. "That's true of me and a lot of things."

"Explain yourself to me."

She scrambled into a sitting position, grabbing the blankets and holding them over her chest. "That doesn't exactly make me feel inspired to share."

"I want to understand you," he said, clearly deciding that there had to be a better way to approach this. "Tell me about yourself. Everything."

"I feel like if you had been paying closer attention you would have deduced the fact that I hadn't been with anybody."

"I assumed you would have found somebody as part of your world travel. Backpacking and staying in hostels generally lends itself to casual hookups."

She drew her knees up to her chest. "You know that from your time spent backpacking?"

"*Everyone* knows that," he said, his tone definitive.

"Okay. Well, I guess this is where I tell you that I'm not like other girls." She laughed. "I mean, obviously. I wasn't raised in a small town. That was misleading. Not entirely a lie, but not entirely the truth. I was raised in a commune."

That was met with nothing but silence.

"You see," she said, "I've learned not to lead with that."

"Do you mean you were raised in a cult?"

"Kind of. I guess. We weren't allowed to watch TV, I wasn't allowed to listen to the radio. I wasn't exposed to any pop culture, any popular music. Nothing. I didn't know anything my family, or the leaders in the community, didn't want us to know."

"That…strangely makes you make more sense." The way he spoke, slowly, as though he were putting all the pieces together and finding out that they did in fact fit, would have been funny if it didn't make her feel like such an oddity.

"I imagine it does." She took a deep breath. "But I never fit. I started…rebelling. Secretly, though, when I was a child."

He stared at her. "When you're raised in one way, believing one thing, exposed to nothing else, what makes you question your surroundings?"

No one had ever asked her that before. Most people didn't want to talk about her past because they found it uncomfortable. Or, they wanted to ask her if she had been a child bride or if she had shaved her head.

"I don't know. I just know that it never felt right. So I started…collecting things. There was a book exchange in the little town we lived near. A wooden kind of mailbox that had free books. And I used to stick them in my bag and sneak them back home when my mom was distracted with her grocery shopping. Then I would take them home and hide them in the woods. I did the same later, with music. But that was harder because I never had much in the way of money. But between rummage sales and the library, I managed to get a portable CD player and some CDs."

"Not a huge rebellion," he said.

"Well, maybe not for everyone. But for me it was. For… for my father it was. My youngest brother is the one who told on me. I know he didn't mean for it to be as bad as it was. I know he didn't mean to… He was just being a brat." She laughed, shaking her head and trying to hold back tears. "He found my books and my music, and he showed my mom. Who in turn showed…my dad. He said I had one chance to say I would never read or listen to anything unapproved again or I…I would have to go."

"And you didn't?" he prompted.

"I wouldn't. So there was a meeting. A meeting with everyone, and I thought…my father loved me. I asked him, I asked him then in front of everyone. If he loved me, how could he send me away just because I liked different books and different music? Just because I was different."

She pressed her hand to her chest, trying to ease the ache. "But he said...he said that if I wouldn't change I couldn't be his daughter anymore. He said it in front of everyone. He said that it was for the good of everyone else. That it was real love to require that I change and...and I don't think it is. It's control. And if he couldn't control me, he didn't want me."

Even though she would never go back, even though she would never make a different decision, it hurt all the same. Her life had changed for the better because she'd left, but she could still never give her father credit for that.

Not when the rejection hurt so much.

"That must have been hard," he said, his voice rough.

"It was," she said. "I felt sorry for myself for a while, then I got a job at a diner in town. Saved up my money for a year. I took the SATs. I got a passport. I went to Europe and started working wherever I could and..."

"And you met Ashley."

"And you," she said, the words settling strangely in the air, tasting strange on her tongue. Settling strangely in her chest. It felt so significant, meeting him. Being here with him. Even though she had decided to have sex with him, knowing that it wasn't about simply experiencing sex, she was still processing the implications of that.

"Yes," he said, something strange coloring his tone. "You got a bit more than you bargained for with all of this, didn't you?" There was something soft in his voice now, and she was suspicious of it. Mostly because there was nothing soft about him.

"You are a lot," she remarked. "A lot of a lot."

"We get along well, don't we?"

"I'm not sure what context you mean that in. You mean, when you're calling me strange and commenting on my habit of eating cereal on the floor?"

"Mostly I mean in bed," he said, "but that is the place I most often try to relate to women."

She frowned. "I'm not sure that was the most flattering thing for you to say."

"I am divorced. You have to consider that there may be a reason for that."

"Well, I met the other half of your marriage. So, I am not terribly mystified as to why that didn't work out. However, I have asked myself a few times why you ended up with her."

"Because she was unsuitable. Because she was a nightmare. And I knew it."

"I don't understand."

"I imagine growing up in a strict household, you received quite a bit of punishment when you did things wrong, or things that your parents thought were wrong."

"Yes," she said, "of course."

"Ashley was my punishment." He laughed, the sound containing no humor at all.

"For what?"

He shook his head. "It doesn't matter." Except, she had a feeling that it mattered more than just about anything else. "But I knew it was doomed. Somewhere, part of me always knew. But you… I feel like with you perhaps things might not be so hopeless."

It felt, very suddenly, as though her stomach had been hollowed out. "What?"

"What if we tried, Esther?"

"Tried what?" She wasn't thinking straight. It was impossible to think straight right now, with their lovemaking still buzzing through her system, with her heart pounding so hard she could scarcely hear her own brain over it.

"Us. Why do we need to separate at the end of this?" He moved closer to her, touching her face, that simple gesture warming her in a way that nothing else ever had. That connection, so desperately needed after being so intimate with him.

"Because," she said, no conviction behind that word whatsoever, "you didn't choose this. Neither did I. We just… We're making the best out of this. And of course we are attracted to each other, but it doesn't make any sense to start in a way that we can't go on."

"That's what doesn't make sense to me. Why can't we go on?"

"You know why. Because I just got away from a restrictive existence. One that made it so I couldn't decide who I was or what I wanted. I can't do that to myself," she said, but still not even she could believe the words coming out of her mouth. She knew in her head that she should, knew that there was truth in them, and that there was importance and weight to what she was doing. Finding herself out here in the real world when before she had been so isolated from it.

And that it was dangerous to feel that everything of importance had shrunk down to this hotel room. To the space between their naked bodies, and the need for there to be less of it.

That her anticipation of what was to come had become small, focused. On where his hand might travel next, what point on her body his fingertips might make contact with next.

So dangerous. So very dangerous.

"Has anything about your life with me been restricting? I have taken you more places than you could have gone on your own. You're not bound to waiting tables in order to stay alive. You have days you could devote to studying, and there is no reason you can't be with me and go to school."

What he was saying… It was so tempting. So bizarrely

clear and easy in appearance in that moment. A life with him, where they could travel at will, where she could still get the schooling that she wanted. It was just that she would be with him. And she couldn't even see that as a negative. Not now, not while her entire being was still humming from his touch.

"But we can't start something that we can't…keep going. I know these babies aren't mine. I went into this knowing that I would give them up. Things are getting muddled, and I don't know if it's hormones or what. I just know that as it gets more real, it gets more difficult. And I just keep telling myself that I can't do it. But do you know what I really can't do? I can't be their mother for a little while and then walk away. I have to either stay as I am, with absolutely no intention of raising them, or I have to have them forever." The very idea made her stomach seize tight with a strange kind of longing.

It was as though a dam had been destroyed and a flood of emotions was suddenly washing forward. Things she hadn't allowed herself to imagine pushing forward in her mind. What it would be like to see the babies once they were born. If she would hold them. And what it would feel like when she did. When they were in her arms rather than in her womb.

What it would feel like to hand them to Renzo and then walk away forever.

Or, even more insidious, what it would feel like to hold them forever. To become a mother.

That thought made her feel like she was being torn in two. Part of her was desperately afraid of having another human life under her care. What did she know? She was practically a child herself, still learning about the world, discovering all of these things that had been hidden from her for so long.

But there was another part of her… Another part of her that craved it in some ways. That craved real connection. Love. In a way she had never before received it in her life. It would be a chance to love someone unconditionally. A chance at having that love returned.

She looked up at Renzo. And that made her feel like she had been shot straight through the heart. Because there was another person involved in all of this, someone other than the children.

She realized then that she wasn't entirely sure what he was suggesting. "Are you suggesting that I stay as the… the nanny? Your mistress? Or…"

"Of course you will be my wife, Esther."

Her stomach tightened painfully. "You want to marry me?"

"We can give our children a family. We can be a family. I made a terrible mistake when I married Ashley. I was angry at the world, I cannot lie to you about that. I was trying to prove something. To prove my lack of worth. But the reality that I am having two children makes me want to do just the opposite. I want to take this situation and turn it into something that could be wonderful for everyone."

This was the first she had heard him express a sentiment like this. But then, this was also the first time they had ever made love. Maybe it had changed things for him, too. She knew that she felt altered. Utterly and completely. Why wouldn't it be the same for him?

But there was one thing she couldn't overlook. She had lived in a household where there was no love, and she knew beyond a shadow of a doubt that she could never do it again. He was promising her things. Promising her freedom, promising her that she could still see to her dreams.

But she needed to know if there was something behind it. If there was insurance. Something to ensure that it wouldn't all break apart, the way that things had broken apart with Ashley and him. Sure, there was the fact that she was not Ashley, but he was still himself. And even though she had feelings for him, deep feelings, there was so much about him she didn't know.

What she felt was much more instinctual than it was logical. There had been something about him, something electric from the moment she had first laid eyes on him. Maybe it was biology. Maybe it had something to do with the fact that she was pregnant with his babies.

But she had a feeling it was deeper.

She wished it weren't deeper. It would make all of this so much simpler. She could evaluate it a bit more coldly. With the sort of distance that it required.

She had no distance.

And she needed to know something, one thing. Because she had learned something important once already. That control was destructive. It had destroyed her mother. Broken her down from the normal woman she'd once been—vibrant and full of life—into a gray and colorless creature. It had very nearly broken her, too. But she'd found the strength to stand.

If she found herself in the same situation again…would she be able to stand strong? Or would she be too damaged, too broken down this time?

No. She couldn't let it. So she had to know.

"Renzo," she said, speaking the words as soon as she could form them in her mind. "I need to know something. I mean, I need to tell you something. I feel like…I've been happy with you these past few weeks. And I didn't expect to be. I didn't even want to be. Because I wanted to feel nothing for you, to feel nothing about this pregnancy. I wanted to be able to walk away. I don't think I can do that now. Not easily. Not the way that I intended. No matter what my intentions were, I know that something has been building between us. That there's a connection there that wasn't before. I think…I think I might love you. And that's why I'm hesitating to say yes to you now. I've lived in a home where I wasn't loved, and I can't do that again. So I need to know. Do you love me? Do you think you could at least grow to love me?"

There was no hesitation. Instead, he leaned forward, kissing her deeply, with all of the lingering passion that still existed between them even after their crashing releases earlier.

"Of course I love you," he said when they parted, his dark gaze intense, as affecting as it had been from the very first moment they'd met. "I want to spend my life with you. Say yes, Esther. Please, say yes."

She looked at him, and she realized that there was only one answer she'd ever given to Renzo, and that would remain true now, too. "Yes," she said, "yes, Renzo. I'll marry you."

# CHAPTER TWELVE

RENZO TOOK A drink and looked out the door of his office, down the darkened hall. He was engaged to Esther now. For real.

And he had lied to her.

There were a great many occasions where he had employed creative truths in order to get his way. It was a necessity in business, and as everyone did it, it seemed as acceptable as anything else. He had done the same with Ashley. From marrying her in Canada to the way he had executed their prenuptial agreement.

He had never felt even the smallest bit of guilt for it. Perhaps because honesty had never gotten him much of anything. Whatever the reasoning, he felt guilty now. He felt guilty lying to Esther.

But would it matter if she never knew? It had cost him nothing to tell her that he loved her. It wouldn't matter one bit that he didn't. She needed to hear it, and that was what mattered.

Except she had told him about her father. About the way he'd controlled her.

He had to wonder how the hell he was any different.

He thought back to the hope shining in her dark eyes, and he crushed the surge of emotion with another slug of alcohol.

They had flown home from New York this morning, and he had done his best to keep his hands off her out of deference to her inexperience. And also, because even he had his limits. He had thought he might keep her mindless and loved up in order to keep her compliance, but that had seemed…distasteful even to him.

However, she seemed happy. She seemed settled in her decision.

And every time she had looked over at him with softness evident in her expression, he had forced himself to continue looking. Had prevented himself from looking away.

And so the guilt had taken even deeper root.

He had lied about a lot of things. But he had never lied about love. He had never once told Ashley that he had feelings for her he didn't have. Not ever.

It shouldn't matter. Because love meant nothing. It had been yanked from his heart by the roots sixteen years ago when his rights to his child had been signed away.

He had forfeited everything then. His right to love. His right to happiness. Even his right to anger. He took another drink.

He set his glass down on the bar with a clink, and then began to walk out of the room, his legs carrying him down the hall and toward Esther. He should stay away from her. He had no right to touch her again. And yet, he was going to.

Of all the things he could not regret that were part and parcel to this deception, it was the fact that he would have possession of her that stood out most. He wanted her. He wanted to keep her near him. Wanted her to live life under his protection, under his care.

*And how are you different from the family she ran away from?*

He was different. He would give her everything she needed. Everything she wanted. In return they would present a compelling picture of family unity to the world, and his children would have a sense of stability. He would inherit the Valenti family company, and as a result, so would the children. Doing anything less would rob them all of that.

There was nothing wrong with that. She would be happy with him.

Everyone would be happier for this decision having been made.

He curled his hand into a fist as he walked down the hall, trying to ignore the intense pressure in his chest.

He remembered her saying something earlier about letting it go. About how she'd had to let go of her past in order to move forward. He didn't know why it echoed in his mind now as he made his way into her bedroom. Perhaps it was because he was longing for her again. Perhaps it was because right now he could feel the weight of it all pressing down on him. All the things that he couldn't bring himself to release his hold on.

Because if he did, what was his life? If he forgot what had created him, then what would fuel him?

He pushed all of that aside, and he embraced the darkness. The darkness that was around him, the darkness that was in him. And he asked himself, not for the first time, what benefit it would be to his children to be raised in such a place, with such a man.

He put his hand to his forehead, pushing back against the tension that was overtaking him. He'd had too much to drink, maybe. That was the only explanation. For both the attack of conscience and the oppressive weight that seemed to assault him now.

"Renzo?"

Esther's voice cut through the darkness. He knew he must look like quite the looming villain, standing in the doorway dimly backlit by the hall. "Yes?"

"Come to bed with me."

That simple offer, so sweet and void of any underlying request, or motive, struck him even harder than it might have considering how deeply he was pondering his own ulterior motives. But he cast them aside now. As he began to cast aside his clothes. He had done the best he could. Keeping his hands off her as though that made him honorable, somehow, when he was manipulating her with his words already.

He had no honor here. He might as well embrace it. He had forgotten why he was even doing this.

He swallowed hard, pulling his shirt over his head then moving his hands to his belt.

"I love you," she said, shifting beneath the blankets and pushing herself into a sitting position. He clenched his teeth, shoving his pants and underwear down and leaving them on the floor. He felt…cold. His chest felt as though it had been wrapped in ice, his heart barely beating now.

He moved slowly to the bed, pressing his knee down on the mattress. Then he leaned forward, his palms flat on each side of her, caging her in. "I love you, too," he said, feeling nothing around his heart when he spoke the words.

He kissed her then, and everything seemed to come to life. All of the ice melting away beneath the heat of the fire that existed between them.

There were a few things that he was certain of in this moment. That she was an innocent. That she deserved better than him. That he was lying. And that he was going to have her anyway.

She moved her hands over his skin, the joy that she seemed to find in exploring his body stoking the flames of his libido and his guilt all at once. All of this was new for her. She'd never had a lover before. Had never even kissed a man before him, and he was going to be the only lover she ever had. Her sexuality would be completely owned by him, utterly shaped by him.

When it came to technique and skill, he supposed she could do worse. He knew that he satisfied her. He knew that he could give her what she wanted. Physically. Emotionally, the exchange would always be empty on his side.

He pushed the thought away. It didn't matter. She would never know. She pushed her fingertips through his hair, clutching his head as he deepened the kiss, as he flattened her against the mattress. She arched against him, a sound of desperation keening through her.

He despised himself then. He was all inside. Thinking all of these things, calculating his every move. And she was honest. Giving. Generous with her body, with her touch. She wiggled beneath him, managing to slip away and push him on to his back at the same time.

"Esther…"

She put her hand at the center of his chest, making a shushing sound as she leaned in and kissed him gently, right against his frozen heart. "Just let me."

She moved lower, blazing a trail down the center of his stomach, farther still until her soft lips brushed up against the head of his arousal.

"Esther," he said, his voice harder than he intended. But he didn't deserve this. Couldn't accept it from her. She was giving him her body this way because she believed there was an emotion that existed between them when it didn't. He was a relatively cold-blooded bastard, but even he had his limits.

Or maybe he didn't.

Because when she parted her lips and enveloped him

in the velvet heat of her mouth, he found he couldn't protest. Not again.

She tasted him as though he were a new delicacy for her to discover. Savored him. Lingered over him in a way that no other woman ever had. She seemed to draw pleasure from his, and that was a new experience. It was strange, to feel this intense, profound attempt at connection coming from someone when he was so accustomed to keeping his walls up at all times.

They were still up. Firmly. But she was testing them.

He wanted to pull away, but he couldn't. Not just because he had to continue on with this pretense, but because he was incapable. Because she held him in thrall, and he could do nothing but submit to the soft, beautiful torture she was lavishing him with.

Fire gathered low in his stomach, and he felt himself nearing the brink of completion. "No," he said, his breath coming out in hard gasps. "Not like that."

He was breathing hard, scarcely in control of his actions, scarcely in control of anything. Trying desperately hard to keep everything together. He was playing a dangerous game with her. And the worst thing he could possibly do was find himself in a position where he began forgetting exactly what he was doing. Exactly what he was trying to accomplish. This wasn't about them. It never had been.

Of course, he wanted her to be happy. But that was incidental. As was she. The only thing that mattered was keeping his children with him. Keeping their family together, keeping Ashley away. The only thing that mattered was building a solid foundation for the rest of his life.

It could be her, it could be any woman. Any woman whom Ashley had chosen, and he would be doing the same thing. He had to remember that. He had to.

On a growl, he pressed her back against the mattress,

claiming her mouth as he tested the entrance to her body with his hard length. She squirmed beneath him, arching into the invasion. And then he thrust deep inside her, all the way home.

His mind went blank then, of everything. Everything but this. This need for release. This need to be as close to her as possible. Everything he had just been telling himself burned away in the white-hot conflagration of need. He gripped her hips as he moved more deeply within her, as he changed the angle and made them both gasp with pleasure.

And then he lost his control completely, and he could only give his thanks when she cried out her release, her internal muscles pulsing around him, because he had lost any and all ability to hold his own at bay. And when it overtook him, it was like a hurricane, pounding over him, consuming him completely, leaving him spent and breathless in the aftermath.

And as he lay there, turmoil and the aftereffects of pleasure chasing each other through his veins, he knew that he was simply in the eye of the storm. It wasn't over.

He moved away from her, shame lashing at him. He hadn't felt quite so remorseful of his actions in a little over sixteen years. Everything was jumbling together. The past, the present, his future. And the reasons for his behavior.

"I'm so happy," Esther said, the bone-deep satisfaction in her voice scraping him raw. So now, she was peaceful, satisfied, and he was… Well, he was nothing of the kind. He felt utterly destroyed. And he couldn't quite figure out why. He had accomplished everything he had set out to accomplish. He had secured a future just like he had set out to do.

Had ensured that he would retain custody of his children, and that they would grow up with the family that they deserved. With the inheritance they deserved, because he was not going to allow his father to divide up Valenti to spite Renzo.

He was confident in these things. Confident that they were right. And she was happy. So nothing else mattered.

"Good," he said.

"But something's bothering me."

"Something is still bothering you? After that orgasm, if anything is still bothering you then I'm going to have to revise my opinion of you. You're a very greedy woman, Esther Abbott."

"I am," she said, nodding slowly, the gesture visible in the darkly lit room. "I want to experience the whole world. And I want to have you while I do it. That's pretty greedy, you have to admit."

"I have offered you both things. So there's no reason you shouldn't want and expect them."

"I want more now."

A surge of anger rocked him. "What exactly would you like, *cara*? The crown jewels, perhaps? What is it that I have denied you exactly that you feel you should have?"

"You," she said simply.

"You just had me. In fact, I find I am spent due to the fact that you had me so well."

"That isn't what I mean. I have a feeling you could share your body endlessly. It's the rest of you that you find difficult."

His chest, frozen before, burned now. "I told you that I loved you," he said, confident those words would end the discussion. "What more could you possibly need?"

"It's really great to hear those words. And I wish that they could be all that I needed. I wish that this could be everything that I needed. But unless I know what's behind it, unless I know what love means to you, how am I supposed to feel? How am I supposed to feel secure in this?

And what we have? We've only known each other for a few weeks. And I feel… I feel so much for you. It's real. But you know where I come from. I feel like I don't know half as much about you."

"You have had dinner with my family. Met my niece. Met my sister. What else do you need to know?"

"Something. Something about you. You said that you married Ashley because you were punishing yourself. To prove something… To prove that you were…bad in some way. I want to understand that. You're angry, Renzo. And I've done my best to ignore that because you've never been angry with me. But I want to know. I want to know what you're angry at. I want to know why you married her. Why marrying me will be different. Why you feel differently about me. I have to. I have to or…"

"You want to know whom I'm angry at?" He pushed himself off the bed, forking his fingers through his hair. "Well, *cara*, there is a very simple answer to that question."

"Give it to me. Give me something."

"Me. I'm angry at me."

# CHAPTER THIRTEEN

ESTHER'S HEART RATE was still normalizing, and hearing those words come out of Renzo's mouth made it tumble over into a strange gear again. She wasn't sure what she had expected when she had demanded that he share something of himself.

Denial, she supposed. Because he was such a closed door she imagined she would have to kick at it more than once in order to get it open.

And so, she was suspicious. She had been growing more and more suspicious ever since their time together in New York. That there was more than he was saying. But he wasn't being as honest or as open as he appeared to be.

She was naive. She knew that. She didn't have experience with men or with romantic relationships, and she knew that it was entirely possible some of her feelings were heightened because of the fact that they were sleeping together.

Except, he hadn't touched her between that first night and tonight. He had been much more careful than she would have liked him to be. Giving her more space than she ever would have asked for.

And in that time all of the tender feelings around her heart hadn't eased. In fact, they had only grown more intense. She knew that there were all kinds of reasons that she might feel something for him that wasn't strictly real.

But with just as much certainty, she knew it was real.

She just wanted it to be real for him, too. She needed to be sure. She had to know. And in order to know, she had to know him.

"Why?" she asked. "Why are you angry at yourself?"

"I wasn't born a debauched playboy. I think that's the place to begin. I was once very sincere, and I believed deeply in love. Though, I perhaps did so in a misguided fashion. But I want to say that so you know I didn't toy with another man's wife as a matter of my own amusement."

Her heart squeezed tight. Another man's wife. If there was a more serious offense she'd heard of in all her growing-up years, she could hardly remember it. Marriage was meant to be sacred. And a man's wife was his. Logically, she knew now that women weren't property, even if they were married. But still, marriage vows were sacred.

"Oh, Renzo... You..."

"It isn't a good story. But then, most origin stories aren't. The man you know isn't one of honor, so you must know that my beginnings were never going to be honorable."

"Don't say things like that. You have honor. Of course you do. Look at everything you're doing to make a life for your children."

"Yes," he said, his tone going utterly flat. "But you have to understand that that need doesn't come from a void. It was born of something. Everything is created. Everyone is created by a defining event. Something that changes you just enough, twists you in your own particular way. You know something about that."

"Yes," she said, thinking of her family.

"My parents care about me. I grew up in privilege. But I made a mistake. I fell in love with the wrong woman. A married woman. She was…my first. My first lover. My first love." He paused, swallowing hard, a muscle in his jaw jumping. "The mother of my child."

Esther felt as though the bottom had fallen away from the bed. She felt as though the bottom had fallen away from the world. She couldn't fathom what he was saying. What he meant. "Your child? But you don't have…"

"Not legally. No. I signed away my parental rights. I have no child. Not as far as the court systems are concerned. Genetically, however, is another matter."

She put her hand to her chest, as if that might do something to still her shattering heartbeat. "Tell me," she said, "tell me everything. How old were you?"

"I was sixteen. And it was agreed there was absolutely no point in a man like me—a boy like me—breaking up a family so that I could… Raise a child? How could I do such a thing? I was nothing more than a child myself. It would be laughable to even think it."

Slowly, realization dawned on her. "That's what you meant. Proving that you were bad. That's why."

"A bit melodramatic, perhaps. But since self-destruction is so much fun, how can I pass up the chance to prove I had no other option? And really, if you look at all of my exploits, how could you possibly believe that I would make a good father?"

"But you will," she said, her tone fierce. "Look at everything you're doing for these children."

He laughed, a bitter sound. "Yes. I'm willing to do anything for these children. Because it is a wound…" His voice broke. "I did what I had to do. I did what I had to do," he said again, as though he were reinforcing it even to himself. "You do not heal from this. You can't. Especially not when…I see her."

"Your ex?"

"No," he said, "I have no lingering feelings for that woman. No attachment to her. I could see her every day and it would make absolutely no difference. But Samantha… My daughter. To watch her grow up across ballrooms, knowing that I can never make contact with her… It is like being stabbed in the same place repeatedly. With no end in sight. The pain never goes away, the wound never heals. There is no chance."

Pain lanced her, for him, for all that he'd been through. For what he still continued to go through, this man who would so obviously sacrifice everything for the love of the children she carried. This man who was already a father, and unable to be with his daughter.

"How old is she?"

"Sixteen," he said. "The same age I was when she was born."

"So," she said, "she's nearly an adult. If you wanted to…"

"And destroy her life? Her view of herself? Her father, her mother, everything? Revealing that she's my child would decimate her entire existence. She has siblings."

"Does her… Does the man who raised her know that she isn't his?"

"I would be surprised if he didn't. I doubt very much he and his wife were ever faithful to each other."

"How did she know it was yours?"

"Jillian had a test done. Mostly because she wanted to make sure it was something I wouldn't contest later. She wanted to know everything. Wanted to make sure that she could protect her marriage. Protect her existing children."

It all made a horrible kind of sense. That it was a situation bound to create casualties. And the solution they had come up with perhaps left the least amount of destruction in its wake. Except when it came to Renzo. As he spoke about it she could see that he had been destroyed entirely over it. That he continued to be destroyed daily.

"You're her father," she said.

He began to pace the length of the room, all restless muscle in the dim light, leashed strength. And she realized it was him all over. Power that he could not wield to its fullest degree. Strength that was impotent in the face of the situation that had been created.

He was a powerful man. He was a wealthy man. But agreements aside, he couldn't go bursting into his daughter's life without destroying the balance. And it was more loving, more gracious, more everything for him to simply stand back and allow himself to bleed so that she never would.

If she hadn't been absolutely certain that she loved him before, this confirmed it. All of her earlier bad feelings about him being with a married woman sort of evaporated. Because he'd made a mistake, but it wasn't who he was.

Except, it had come to define him. Because the consequence was so permanent.

She couldn't continue to punish him by holding it against him. She couldn't hold any of this against him. She looked at him and she saw the man she was determined to make a life with. A man who was angry, injured, broken beyond anything she could possibly understand.

What could she offer him?

"I am not her father in any way that counts," he responded.

"But you are," she said. "You love her. Maybe more than anyone else involved in this, because the only reason that you've never crossed that ballroom and put yourself in her life is that you love her too much to rattle her."

"No," he said, his tone fierce. "It's not love. I can't feel that way anymore. I don't."

Those words hit her like a hammer fall. "But you said… You said you loved me."

"And if it makes you happy I will say it a thousand more times."

"If it makes me *happy*. But… What about if it's not true?"

"I am who I am. What has been done to me… It is done. There is no going back. I cannot go back in time and make a different decision. I can't change what happened. Not me, not her. I can't remake that decision. Don't you understand that? And just like I can't remake that decision, I can't feel things with parts of myself that I burned away. It doesn't work that way. It can't."

"Then why did you tell me that?"

"Have you been listening?" he asked, roaring now, when she had only ever heard him speak in calm command before. There was no sense of calm about him now. It was like watching him unravel in front of her, thread by thread. "I will do anything to keep my children with me. Anything."

"I never threatened to take them. Ever. I wouldn't. I wouldn't do that to you."

"It's more than that. Samantha… She has a family. She has a mother and she has a father. How could I provide less to my children now? What is my excuse? Look what I did. I ruined my life by marrying Ashley. I will not ruin my children's lives. I was making a statement, about my unsuitability, and I nearly swept two innocent children up in that. My own children. Again. Ruined by the selfishness of the adults around them."

She could see it so clearly. The way that he did. That he was somehow building the family that he owed his children so he didn't give them less than what his first child had been given.

He had tried so hard to prove that he wasn't able. To prove that the right decision had been made, and then he had been thrust into a situation where he had to prove himself worthy.

But she had been caught in the crossfire. And understanding it didn't make her any less confused when it came to her own feelings. It didn't make it hurt less.

"You didn't have to lie to me," she said.

"I did. You made that very clear."

"Renzo…I…I gave myself to you. In a way that I don't know if I could have if…" She stopped then, because she knew it wasn't true. It had nothing to do with the way he felt, the way that she had been with him earlier. It had everything to do with the way that she felt. With how much she felt for him. But still, she was hurt, she was confused, and she wanted him to feel even a fraction of that, which wasn't really fair considering she had a feeling he had been awash in both from the moment he had found out she was carrying his children.

And she could see fear in his eyes. Stark, naked. The fear that somehow, another woman would contrive to take away what he wanted most in the world. And he might say he couldn't love, but his actions were not those of a man who couldn't love.

She knew this was all about love. Deep, unending love that hurt him every time his heart beat.

If he thought he was doing this out of a lack of love, it was only because he couldn't see another way to deal with it. And strangely, she understood that. It was easy to tell herself that she was staying with him because he said he loved her. Because she was having these babies.

Far scarier was to admit to herself that it was something

she wanted. To be with him because she cared. Because she was choosing it.

It was one thing to make a distinction between her father and Renzo in theory. And to make a case for signing herself up for something completely different from what she had imagined she would do with her life. To sign on for binding herself to a man who certainly had his own agenda and his own idea about things.

Because he had lied to her. And what if she was just walking into the same kind of thing again? To living a life dictated by somebody else. That scared her. But maybe… Maybe love was always scary.

Maybe it was a risk, and it was one that came with sacrifice, with cost.

That thought made her feel panic. She had sacrificed so much. To stay with her family as long as she had, she had ignored so much of herself that she wanted to explore. She had tried so hard to be everything her mother and father had wanted her to be.

And leaving… If leaving her siblings had been painful, just thinking about what might happen if she was forced to leave these children made her insides ache.

Renzo was a rock wall. And she was just so very soft and breakable, no matter how much she might want to fling herself against him and see if she could force a crack. Force a change.

To see if she could get to what she suspected was behind it.

But how could she do that if not even he would admit that it was there? If not even he seemed to know?

"I didn't mean to hurt you," he said. "But I'm never going to love you the way that you seem to want me to. But that doesn't mean I won't be a faithful husband. I was a faithful husband to Ashley in spite of the fact that she wasn't faithful to me. If you need a demonstration, I will even marry you here. In Italy. Where divorce will be difficult to achieve."

All of these promises, all of these things, she recognized as things that benefited him more than they did her. At the end of the day, if there was ever any genetic testing done, a judge would find that the children didn't belong to her. And then what?

Everything had changed so much in the past few weeks. Her life looked like an entirely different one from what she had imagined she would make for herself.

Had it been only four months since she had imagined that she would do the surrogacy and then walk away? That she would go on to go to school and visit exotic places, and do all of these things she had dreamed about without ever once thinking about the children she had given birth to again? Without ever once thinking of Renzo again. She knew now that none of that was possible.

She had trapped herself. Utterly and completely.

Out of the frying pan and into the fire. She couldn't even decide if she wanted out of the fire.

"You did hurt me," she said, choosing to ignore what he'd said about marriage and divorce, forcing him to discuss the lie. The lie that was, by seconds, growing bigger and bigger inside her.

Because it had been the difference. The difference between captivity and a relationship. The difference between a controlling, autocratic man and a caring, invested man.

Yes, in all of those scenarios he had done the same things, but if he did them from a position of love, if he did them out of caring for her, caring for the babies, it was different from simply wanting to make his life easier.

"That wasn't my intention. It doesn't have to change

things between us. You want me." He moved nearer to her, his fingertips brushing over her cheekbone, and much to her eternal humiliation, a shiver of need worked its way through her.

"It's not enough." She jerked away from him, shrinking back toward the headboard.

"Why not?" he asked, his tone fraying.

"I want you to be with me," she said, speaking slowly, trying to figure out a way to articulate what she was feeling, not just to him but to herself. "I want you to be with me because it makes me feel stronger. It makes me feel weaker. Because you make me want things I didn't even know a person could want. Because you make my body hum and my heart beat faster." She closed her eyes. "I thought I knew what I wanted. I thought I knew what I needed. Then I met you and I had to question all of it. I met you and looked at your eyes and found I couldn't move. Found that I didn't even want to. It's not convenient for me, Renzo. Nothing about this is. I don't want you because it makes my life easier. I don't want you because of everything you can give me, but because of all the little ways you have changed me. Because you hollowed me out and created a need that I didn't know existed before. And none of it's convenient. Not in the least. But it's that lack of convenience that makes me so sure it's real."

"But why does it matter?" he asked again. "We can be happy here. You can feel all of those things. We will be together, this whole family will be together."

"What do you feel when you touch me?"

"I want to have you."

Her throat tightened. "And when you think of me leaving you?"

He closed the space between them then, grabbing hold

of her arms and holding on to her tightly. "You won't. I want to keep you."

She reached up, brushing her fingertips over his cheek lightly. "And that's the difference. You want to keep me because it makes your life more the picture that you want. Because it's good for a man to have a wife, for his children to have a mother. But don't you understand, that's the exact reason my father wanted me to stay. The reason that he treated his children the way he did. Because he needed that picture. That perfect picture. Because it was about the way it made everyone look at him. About wanting to possess a perfect image." She swallowed hard. "I can't be someone else's trophy. I can't be the evidence of their perfect life lived. Not again. Not when it took so much strength to leave it the first time. Because if you're only telling me you love me to make me happy, then it's just more control."

"That isn't fair," he ground out. "I'm not talking about denying you anything. I'm not hiding the world from you. I have promised you an education. I have promised to show you all of life. All that the world has to offer."

"I know. I do…"

"Am I a selfish lover?"

Her cheeks heated. "No. Of course you aren't."

"How dare you compare me to the man who spent your life controlling you. It is different. It is different to come to an understanding based on mutual convenience, mutual attraction."

She lay down, letting misery overtake her, drawing her knees up to her chest and turning away from Renzo. "I need space," she said, feeling like her head was teeming with noise. She wasn't sure she'd ever be able to cut through it.

"I will see you at breakfast," he said, his tone hard.

She listened for him to leave the room. Didn't move again until she heard the door to his room close down the hall. And then she let the first sob rack her body.

She felt raw. Deceived. She felt foolish, because she had done exactly what inexperienced women did. She had believed him when he'd said he loved her, and she had used it as a shield. That lie had made her feel impenetrable. Had made her feel as though she could do anything, be anything.

And now, she just felt like a fool.

There was also something gnawing at the back of her mind. About the comparison she had made between Renzo and her father. About her life spent in the commune, and the month she had spent here.

She had known she wanted to escape that life. She had always felt like her home was a prison. She didn't feel that now, and she didn't know what that said about her. She wasn't even sure she cared.

She made a low, miserable sound and buried her face in her pillow. She didn't want to leave him. It didn't matter that he said he didn't love her. She wanted to be here. Wanted to be with him.

It had nothing to do with what he felt, and everything to do with what she felt. Her love wasn't a lie. Even his admission hadn't shaken it.

But it still confused her. Still made her feel like she had to do something, had to change something. To avoid becoming the sad, controlled creature she had once been.

"I don't want to," she said into the stillness of the room, a tear sliding down her cheek. She wanted to stay here with him. She wanted to make a life with him, and their children. She wanted him to have what he craved.

But for how long? How long would it take for her to start to feel smothered again?

What had felt like absolute freedom before felt like prison now. And regardless of her confused feelings on whether or not she wanted to leave, she felt trapped now when before she had felt liberated.

It was so easy to see the difference. Love. Love was the difference.

Knowing Renzo didn't love her, knowing that he never could, made all the difference to her.

# CHAPTER FOURTEEN

RENZO SLEPT LIKE absolute hell. He felt every inch like the ass that he was. The things he had said to Esther. The way that he had hurt her. He had lied to her, it was true. Everything he had been through surrounding the loss of Samantha had done something to him. Changed him. If he had emerged from it with an edge of ruthlessness, no one could blame him.

Because he had been involved in a situation where he had allowed others to dictate things for him. But he resisted that now, more than anything. Resisted allowing anyone or anything to have the upper hand when he needed it at all times.

Still, Esther had not deserved his lies. If there was anyone truly good and sweet in the world, it was her. Anyone who had already been badly used by controlling men.

He slammed his cup of coffee down on the table and turned, seeing her standing at the bottom of the stairs. "Good morning," he said.

"Good morning," she said, shifting. And that was when he noticed her backpack.

She was back in her old clothes, too. Wearing a tight black tank top and the long flowing skirt, her stomach so much rounder than it had been when he'd first met her.

And he knew. Just what she was doing.

"You cannot leave," he said, his voice like shattered glass in the still surroundings.

"I have to," she said. "I'm not leaving town. I promise. But I can't stay here with you. Not while I'm so confused. I don't know what's going to happen between us, and I don't know…I don't know how I feel. I can't sit here where I'm comfortable, where I'm close to you, and think straight. And I owe myself the chance to think straight."

He was dimly aware of crossing the space between them, of taking her in his arms, much more roughly than he might have done if he were thinking straight. "You cannot leave me."

"I can. And I need to. Please, you have to understand."

He took hold of her wrists, backing her against the wall and pinning her there, looking deep into her eyes because she had said once that his looking at her had changed something. He needed to change it now. Needed to immobilize her now. Needed to stop her from leaving him.

"You can't go," he said again, more forcefully this time.

"Renzo," she said, "you can't keep me here. You don't want a prisoner. Mostly because you know that I've been one. You wouldn't do that to me, not again."

Desperation clawed him like an animal. In this moment, he was unsure if there was a limit to what he would do. Because he was about to watch his entire life, his future, walk out the door and away from him. "How can you do this to me?" he asked. "You know my past. You know what I have lost. I entrusted that secret to you. No one knows. My sister doesn't even know. And I told you."

"I will never take your children from you. I told you that already. I'm not going to take your chance to be a father. But…I don't believe that the two of us living together without love is going to give them a better childhood. I just don't. I grew up in a house that didn't have love. Where all of the relationships were so…unhealthy. And filled with control. It isn't going to help your children to live that way."

"Is the real issue that you want to leave? That you want to walk away? That you don't want to deal with this thing between us?"

"No."

"You feel your life will be hampered by raising children. You don't actually want the babies." That would almost make it easier. Because he would not expose children to her indifference. Though, he could not imagine Esther expressing indifference toward a puppy, much less a baby.

"This is about you and me," she said, pressing her hand to his face. She didn't struggle against his hold. She simply touched him, gently, with a kind of deep emotion he could not recall anyone ever pouring out over his skin. "About what we're supposed to be. That's all. I can't marry you. Not like this. I can't sign on to a life of being unloved."

She began to move away from him then, and he tightened his hold on her, desperation like a feral creature inside him.

"I love you," he ground out, the words coming from deep within his soul.

Suddenly, he was overcome by a sensation that all of the blood had drained from his head. That he couldn't breathe. That he might fall to the ground, black out, lose consciousness. And he was forced to come to the conclusion that it was because it was true.

That for the first time in his memory he loved a person standing in front of him more than the breath in his own body. That he loved her, in spite of his best efforts not to.

"I love you," he said again, desperation making it sharp.

"Renzo," she said, taking a step back. And he let her. "Don't do this to me. Don't lie to me. Don't use my feelings against me."

"I'm not," he said. "This is the truth."

"You already told me that you would tell me you loved me a thousand times if it would make me happy. I imagine you would say it a thousand more if you thought it would help you get your way. But I can't live that way. I won't."

"I won't live without you," he said, those words making her pause.

She turned back to face him. "When you can tell me what has changed because you love me, when you can prove to me that this isn't just another lie. When you can prove to me this isn't just you trying to keep ownership... Then you come find me. I'm going back to the bar. I'm going back to the hostel."

Then suddenly he was driven by the impulse to hurt. The wound as bad as if he was being injured. To make her bleed, because he damn sure was. "Run away, then. And tell yourself whatever story you need to tell yourself. About your bid for freedom. But this is just more of the same selfishness you showed when you left your family," he spat. "If somebody doesn't love you in exactly the way you wish them to, you don't recognize it. And you say it isn't real. Isn't that the same as your father? You accuse me of being selfish, Esther, but at least I took you at face value. You will not do the same for me."

She flinched, and he could tell that the words had hit their mark. That they had struck her in a place where her fear lived. Fear that what he said might be true.

"Maybe you're right. Except, I never lied to you. So maybe this is the one thing you'll never be able to get over, maybe this is my betrayal to you that you won't be able to let go. But yours was the first lie. How will I ever know if the words that come out of your mouth are real? How? You told me you loved me without flinching the first time. And then you told me it was all a lie, and now you ask me to believe that this is true. You ask impossible things of me, Renzo. I just wanted to see the world." She wiped at a tear that had fallen down her cheek. "I just wanted to go to a university and find myself. I didn't want to be broken. Not again. And that's what you've done. So now I have to go put myself back together again, and if you can come to me and show me, then please do. But if not... Leave me alone. I'll keep you informed about the doctor's appointments."

She moved to the door, holding on to her backpack tightly. "Goodbye, Renzo."

And then she was gone. And for the second time in his life Renzo felt like he was watching his entire future slip through his fingers. For the second time, he felt powerless to do anything about it.

When Renzo went to visit his father later that day, he was full of violent rage. Ever since Esther had walked out of his home, he had been angry, growing angrier. Ever since she had left him, the fire of rage had been burning hotter and hotter in the pit of his stomach.

It had fueled him, spurred him with a kind of restless energy that he couldn't control. And it had brought him here. His parents' home.

He walked into his father's office without knocking.

"Renzo," his father said, without looking up. "What brings you here?"

"I have something to tell you," Renzo said.

"I do hope that you've already married that woman. Because I would hate to hear that things had gone awry."

"Oh, it's gone awry. The entire thing is damn well sideways."

"Do you need me to intervene? Is that it? God knows it's what I did when your last youthful indiscretion—"

"My youthful indiscretion? You mean my daughter? My

daughter I'm not allowed to see, because you, mother and Jillian decided that it would be better that way?"

"As if you didn't believe the same. You were sixteen years old. You couldn't have raised the child. Your behavior over the last several years has proved as much."

His father said that as though it were accidental. As though it never occurred to him that Renzo had perhaps engineered his behavior around proving that very thing. But then, he supposed he couldn't blame his father for that. Not even Renzo had fully realized that until recently. Until he'd been forced to change what he was, what he wanted, so that he could seize the opportunity to be a father this time around.

"There is nothing youthful about this indiscretion," Renzo said. "I am not a child. I'm a man in his thirties. And beyond that, the situation is not as it appears."

"What is going on?"

"It's Ashley. Ashley struck up an agreement with Esther. Esther agreed to carry my children as a surrogate. Of course, I was not consulted about any of this. And then when Ashley decided that the pregnancy was not going to preserve our marriage, she contacted Esther and asked that Esther have the pregnancy terminated. She didn't want to do that. Instead, she came to me." He rubbed his hand over his face. "I lost one child, and I was bound and determined to hold on to this one. To these two," he amended, an arrow hitting him in the heart as he thought of his twins. "I was also determined to do as you said. To prevent any other scandal. Anything that might come back and hurt them. I was not going to allow my brother-in-law to get control of the company, not when it's the rightful inheritance of my children. As much as you might have hoped you were appealing to my selfishness, believe me when I say you were simply appealing to my desire to give my children everything they deserve this time around."

"I cannot believe this. It isn't true. Such a thing isn't even legal in this country."

"There are ways to circumvent legality, as I'm sure you know. But now I have ruined everything with Esther. And I have done so in part because I was letting you control things again."

"You say all of this as though you're angry about what I did back then."

"I am. I damn well am. I was sixteen, I didn't know. I didn't know what I would feel. Every time I look across the room I see her. Every time. It is like being stabbed straight through the heart. I cannot forgive myself for the decision that I made then. I cannot forgive you for the part that you played in it."

His father pounded his fist down on his desk. "That feeling that you have I have for you. Magnified with an intensity that you cannot possibly imagine. Because I raised you. Because you are the heir to everything that I have worked so hard to build. My hope is placed in you, Renzo. You are everything to me in more ways than you can know. I did what I had to do to protect you, and if I have earned your anger then I accept that. But I would not change what I did."

His father's words struck him hard. Along with the realization that while he could understand why the decision had been made, he still wished he could change it.

"Do you not think it hurts me?" his father asked, his voice rough. "Because I see her, too. She is my granddaughter. And especially since your sister had Sophia, I feel that loss. The loss of my first grandchild that I cannot acknowledge."

"But it was not as important to you as protecting the family reputation."

"The greater good," he said. "And it so happened that it also protected her mother's marriage. That entire family. You cannot claim that I am so selfish, Renzo."

"Still, you wanted me to marry Esther to preserve your reputation. I imagine you want to keep the circumstances around the conception of the babies a secret, as well."

"Do you suggest that putting all of it out in the open is for the best? What about the reputation of the Valenti family?"

"I don't know," he said, tapping the back of the chair that was placed in front of his father's desk. "I don't know. But I cannot protect the reputation of the Valentis. Not at the expense of my own life. Not at the expense of the people I love."

"And the love of your parents? Does that not figure into this at all?"

"You can protect yourself, Father. I think you're more than able. My children cannot. They are helpless. They are depending on me to make the right choice."

"And you think bringing them into the world under a cloud of scandal is the right thing to do?"

"I am tired of lies. I am tired of living a life built on a monument to the one thing I can never acknowledge. The one person I will always love that I can never acknowledge. I am tired of living in an existence that is an unholy altar to my failures. Confirmation that I had no other choice. No other choice but to give up Samantha when I did. And perhaps then it was true. But I have choices now. And perhaps I will humiliate myself. Perhaps I will humiliate our family. But if I have to do that to win back the woman I love, if I have to stop protecting myself in every way in order to prove my vulnerability, then I will do it. If the perfect reputation of our family is a casualty, then I accept it. But I will not be a slave to it." He let out a harsh breath, Esther, her lie, her story on his mind. "I can't control everything. I'll only end up breaking everything I care about."

"I did what I had to do," his father said. "I counseled you the way that I had to. I am the patriarch of this family, Renzo. Protecting it is my highest calling."

"Perhaps that is the problem. And where we have reached an impasse. Because I am the patriarch of my family. My family, which is Esther and the children she's carrying. I lost her. I lied to her, and I told her I could never love her. I was afraid, afraid because I could not subject myself to the kind of pain that I went through, the kind of pain I continually go through, where Samantha is concerned. But all I've done is made it worse. And I'm going to fix it. No matter what."

He turned, getting ready to walk out of the office. He stopped when his father spoke.

"Renzo. I might not agree with the decision you're making, but I do want you to know that I understand I can't protect you now. Moreover, that you don't need me to. You're a man now, a man who has understandable anger directed at me. I only hope that someday you will forgive me."

Renzo let out a hard breath, and he thought of something else Esther had said. About how she'd had to let go of the past to truly move forward.

He had one foot firmly in the past, and it had nearly ruined everything. He had to start walking forward. Forward to Esther.

"I imagine," he said, "that will all depend on what happens next."

# CHAPTER FIFTEEN

ESTHER FELT DRAINED. Emotionally, physically. Going back to work at the bar was difficult now. Her stomach was bigger, her ankles were bigger, her fatigue was bigger. Plus, all she wanted to do was crawl underneath the bar and cry for the entire shift, because something inside her felt fundamentally broken since she'd walked away from Renzo.

It was oppressively humid tonight. And hot. Clouds had rolled in, and she had a feeling there was going to be a late-evening thunderstorm, the impending rain adding to the heaviness in the atmosphere. Adding to the heaviness in her heart.

She looked outside and saw drops begin to pound the cobbled sidewalk. Great. Walking home was going to be fun. All of her clothes would be stuck to her skin. Then she would spend the rest of the evening shivering, because the showers in the hostel never had enough hot water to get rid of a chill like this once it soaked into her bones.

A flash of lightning split the sky, and she jumped a little bit. "Esther?"

She turned and saw her boss, who was gesturing madly at the tables outside. She knew that he wanted her to bring in the seat covers. "Okay," she said.

She hurried outside, not bothering to put on a sweater or anything. The air was still warm, but the drops falling from the sky were big and aggressively cold. She hunched over, taking hold of the cushions, collecting them beneath her arm.

Suddenly, the back of her neck prickled and she straightened slowly. Another flash of lightning washed out the scene around her, and that was when she saw him. Renzo, standing there in a suit just as he had done that first night he had come to the bar.

He was standing in a suit, in the rain, water pouring down over him, his hands in his pockets, his dark eyes trained on her.

"What are you doing here?" she asked, the cushions suddenly tumbling from her arms. She hadn't even realized she had released her hold on them.

It was the same as it had always been. From the beginning. Those dark eyes rooting her to the spot, her entire world shifting around her, shifting around him.

Everything changed, even the air. If he had brought the thunderstorm with him, she wouldn't be surprised.

"I came to see you. You told me to come and find you when I was ready. When I was ready to prove this to you. To prove my love. And I am. Trust me, I was tempted to hold a press conference before I came to see you, but I did feel like I should talk to you first. Not for me. But for you."

"A press conference? What kind of press conference?"

"To explain. Everything. The surrogacy… Everything. Because, I thought maybe if I didn't have a reputation to protect anymore you wouldn't be able to accuse me of being motivated by it."

"I…I suppose it's easy for me to say when nobody is interested in me or my life. At least, not apart from you."

"Don't excuse yourself," he said, "not now. You were right about me. It was all about doing something that suited me, and I want to make sure that this no longer does. I want to make sure that I'm no longer doing everything with a view of creating a smooth facade over my life. All of that… It is the reason that I am the way I am now. And my dedication to it was to justify my earlier actions. But no more. I am prepared to go public with our story. To let everyone know that you are a surrogate, and that I was fooled by my ex-wife."

"But what about all the legality?"

He took a deep breath. "That's why I didn't have the press conference. I was afraid that you would be concerned I was using it to lessen your claim on the babies. That I was using it to try to make sure you didn't have a place in their life. So you see, even with the desire to enact a grand gesture, I'm somewhat hampered by the fact that I have an unequal amount of power here." He shook his head. "But only on the outside. Inside… Inside I'm trembling. Because I don't know how to make you believe me. Because I haven't earned the right to have you do it."

He moved closer to her, and she watched him come. The rain pelted her skin, her clothes completely plastered to her body. She didn't care. "My father told me that I had to make sure everything went right this time. That I had to keep the family together or he was going to take my inheritance from me. I understand that only puts another nail in the coffin of my sincerity, but please understand that in part I was motivated by the desire to keep all of the inheritance for my children."

"So, your father told you to marry me."

He nodded. "Yes, and it was the thing that pushed me to make it real. And then that first night we were together, I saw Samantha. And I knew… Whatever I had to do I would do it. Including lie to you. And that's the hardest thing, Esther. It is the hardest thing to come back from, because you know me. You know that I would do anything for my children. And I have proved to you that I'm willing to lie. But I thought for certain that I had already experienced the lowest moments life had to offer. How could I not? I watched my child grow up a stranger to me. But I was wrong. There is lower."

She hurt for him. Physically hurt. But she found that she needed to hear it. Needed to hear about the pain he'd been through, because he had hurt her so profoundly. "What was it?"

"Telling you that I loved you, knowing that it was true this time, and knowing there was nothing I could do to convince you. Knowing that I had destroyed that chance already. That I had taken something beautiful, wonderful—love and the ability to feel it—and turned it into a farce. That I had finally found that feeling and myself again, and that I wanted it, and that I had destroyed any chance of getting it in return."

She couldn't take it anymore. She couldn't hold back. She moved to him, wrapping her arms around him, letting the rain pelt them both, washing away all of the hurt that was between them. "I believe you," she said. "I do. And you haven't squandered anything. I love you. And I knew that you could love me. I did. Because the way that you rearranged your life so that you could be a father to these children, the way that you spoke about the pain you felt over Samantha, the way you continue to feel pain because you won't do anything to disturb her, that's love, Renzo. That's real love. Sacrificial love, not controlling love."

"I wanted to pretend that it wasn't there, because it was easier. Admitting that you love someone when you know you can never be with them in the way that you want to be is a terrible fate. I experienced that with Samantha. And then with you."

"I love you. I'm here. You don't have to prove anything

to me. I'm so touched that you were willing to do that, but I think it's probably for the best if we don't make our children a headline."

"Probably so," he said, sliding his hand down her back. "I love you, Esther. And what love has always meant to me has been something distant. From my father it was control. And with my daughter it was a required separation. You asked me what love was, and when it comes to loving someone and being with them, I'm not sure I know. But I want to learn. That is what I can offer you. My willingness to change. To be changed by this thing between us, in more ways than I already have been."

"I suppose that's fair," she said, sniffling. "I don't really know what it is either. All of my life it meant control, too. And I left home looking for something. Freedom. I thought that it would come with travel, with education, with no one to hold me back or tie me down. And that is a kind of freedom. But it's incomplete. I met you, I started to have feelings for you, and it made me ache. It made me want. It wasn't easy. Deciding to be a mother to twins when I had been planning on something else entirely isn't easy. But what I've learned spending these last couple of years alone is that things are easier when you don't care. The more you care the more it costs. We both know that. I would rather care. And I would rather have all of the painful things that go with that so that I can have the real, joyous things that go along with it, too. I would rather do that than drift along easily. And I would rather do it with you."

He cupped her chin, tilting her face up and kissing her, water drops rolling over their skin as he continued to taste her, as he sipped the moisture from her mouth.

"I'm going to get fired," she said.

"Well, it's a good thing you're going to marry a billionaire."

"Arrogant. I didn't say I would marry you. I just said that I loved you."

"I am arrogant. That is part of loving me, you will find."

"Well, I'll probably still eat cereal on the floor. That is part of loving me."

A smile curved his lips. "I want all the parts of loving you. From the flat shoes to the cereal, to the pain in my chest when I think of what it would mean to lose you. I want to teach you about the world, and I want you to teach me how to be a better man. How to be the man you need."

Thunder rolled through the air, through her chest, the bass note that seemed to match the intensity of the love inside her. "Renzo, don't be silly. You're already the man I need. You were, from that first moment I saw you. You're not the man I would have chosen, but you are the one I love. You are the one I needed. I wanted freedom, I wanted to see everything of the world, but believe me when I tell you I have never felt so free than when you're holding me. The world that we create between us is the most beautiful one I could have ever imagined."

"Even when I am overbearing? And impossible?"

She nodded, unable to hold back the smile that stretched her lips wide. "Even then. Because, you see, Mr. Valenti, the thing is I love you. And if you love me then everything else is just window dressing."

"I do love you, Esther. We may have had a strange beginning, but I think we're going to have the happiest ending."

"So do I, Renzo. So do I."

# EPILOGUE

IT WAS AN interesting thing, to go from a family where love had been oppressive, to one where it was the very air Esther breathed.

But after five years with Renzo, their twins and two other children, plus nieces and nephews and her in-laws, Esther felt freer than she ever had. Surrounded, and yet liberated.

Renzo's parents were not the easiest people, but they loved him and their grandchildren with a very real ferocity that was irresistible to Esther.

She had become very good friends with her sister-in-law, Allegra, and her husband, Cristian. They had spent many long dinners laughing together while the children played.

The only thing that ever bothered Esther was the fact that she couldn't heal Renzo's every wound. He loved her, he loved their children. And he did it with absolutely no reservation. But still, Esther knew that he wondered about his oldest child, the one he had never gotten to know.

Until, one day a letter came in the mail. From Samantha. Somehow, she had found out about her origins and had decided to contact Renzo. Because she wanted to know her father, the man who had given her up quietly so that her family wouldn't be disturbed.

For Esther, it hadn't been a difficult thing to allow Samantha into their family. It had never even occurred to her to close the door on the daughter who meant so much to her husband. Still, one night after a visit from Samantha, Renzo pulled her into his arms and kissed her.

"Thank you," he said, "thank you so much for accepting her like you have. What we have here is so complete, and I know that adding more to it can be difficult…"

"No," she said, pressing her fingers to his lips. "It isn't difficult. Nothing about loving you has ever been difficult, and seeing you with all the pieces of your heart back in place is the most beautiful gift I could have ever been given."

Her husband's eyes were suspiciously bright when he went to kiss her again. And then he said in a husky voice, "The most beautiful gift I have ever been given was you. Without you, I would have none of this. Without you I would still be a debauched playboy who had absolutely everything except the one thing he needed."

"What's that?"

"Love, Esther. Without you, I would have no love. And with you my life is full of it."

Then he carried her upstairs and proceeded to show her just how little control he had where she was concerned, and just how much he loved her. And Esther never doubted— not once—that Renzo's love was the absolute truth.

\* \* \* \* \*

*Don't miss the first two stories in*
*Maisey Yates's* HEIRS BEFORE VOWS *trilogy*

THE SPANIARD'S PREGNANT BRIDE
*and*
THE PRINCE'S PREGNANT MISTRESS
*Available now!*

# MILLS & BOON®

# MODERN™

**POWER, PASSION AND IRRESISTIBLE TEMPTATION**

7/01

# MILLS & BOON®

## EXCLUSIVE EXTRACT

Even unsentimental Alessandro Di Sione can't deny
his grandfather's dream of retrieving a scandalous
painting. Yet its return depends on outspoken Princess
Gabriella. Travelling together to locate the painting,
Gabby is drawn to this guilt-ridden man.
Could their passion be his salvation?

*Read on for a sneak preview of*
*THE LAST DI SIONE CLAIMS HIS PRIZE*

Alessandro was so different than she was. Gabby had
never truly fully appreciated just how different men and
women were. In a million ways, big and small.

Yes, there was the obvious, but it was more than that.
And it was those differences that suddenly caused her to
glory in who she was, what she was. To feel, if only for
a moment, that she completely understood herself both
body and soul, and that they were united in one desire.

"Kiss me, Princess," he said, his voice low, strained.

He was affected.

So she had won.

She had been the one to make him burn.

But she'd made a mistake if she'd thought this game
had one winner and one loser. She was right down there
with him. And she didn't care about winning anymore.

She couldn't deny him, not now. Not when he was
looking at her like she was a woman and not a girl, or
an owl. Not when he was looking at her like she was

the sun, moon and all the stars combined. Bright, brilliant and something that held the power to hold him transfixed.

Something more than what she was. Because Gabriella D'Oro had never transfixed anyone. Not her parents. Not a man.

But he was looking at her like she mattered. She didn't feel like shrinking into a wall, or melting into the scenery. She wanted him to keep looking.

She didn't want to hide from this. She wanted all of it.

Slowly, so slowly, so that she could savor the feel of him, relish the sensations of his body beneath her touch, she slid her hand up his throat, feeling the heat of his skin, the faint scratch of whiskers.

Then she moved to cup his jaw, his cheek.

"I've never touched a man like this before," she confessed.

And she wasn't even embarrassed by the confession, because he was still looking at her like he wanted her.

He moved closer, covering her hand with his. She could feel his heart pounding heavily, could sense the tension running through his frame. "I've touched a great many women," he said, his tone grave. "But at the moment it doesn't seem to matter."

That was when she kissed him.

*Don't miss*
THE LAST DI SIONE CLAIMS HIS PRIZE
By Maisey Yates

Available February 2017
www.millsandboon.co.uk